Weiss rifled through the beakers and bottles in a panic, checking every label in sight, looking for the VX411 vaccine. With each passing moment, his movements grew less sure—and more dangerous. Overhead, Bergin's useless siren continued to wail, a perfectly psychotic sound track for Sydney's current situation. Each rise and fall of the alarm raised her tension level higher.

"Weiss," Sydney shouted. Her own hands were working furiously, checking the vials on the first table. Any second, another troop of guards could burst in on them, making the task at hand even more difficult.

Weiss dropped a vial but grabbed it before it could roll off the table and smash on the floor. He put it back in its grid, took a deep breath, and kept searching. This was not good.

"Weiss!" Sydney shouted again. "You have to get out of here!"

Either ignoring her or unable to hear, Weiss turned from his table and started to search the next one. Sydney's heart pounded with trepidation and pity. He was fearing for his life.

Also available from

SIMON SPOTLIGHT ENTERTAINMENT

ALIAS

THE
apo
SERIES

TWO OF A KIND?

FAINA

COLLATERAL DAMAGE

ALIAS™

THE SERIES

REPLACED

ALIAS™

THE SERIES

REPLACED

EMMA HARRISON

An original novel based on the
hit TV series created by J. J. Abrams

SSE

SIMON SPOTLIGHT ENTERTAINMENT
New York   London   Toronto   Sydney

SᴉSᴉE

SIMON SPOTLIGHT ENTERTAINMENT
An imprint of Simon & Schuster
1230 Avenue of the Americas, New York, New York 10020
Text and cover art copyright © 2005 by Touchstone Television
All rights reserved, including the right of reproduction in whole or in part in any form.
SIMON SPOTLIGHT ENTERTAINMENT and related logo are trademarks of Simon & Schuster, Inc.
Manufactured in the United States of America
First Edition 10 9 8 7 6 5 4 3 2 1
Library of Congress Control Number 2004117773
ISBN-13: 978-1-4169-0246-1
ISBN-10: 1-4169-0246-5

CHAPTER 1

"Where is this guy? Doesn't he realize this is supposed to be *his* party?"

Sydney Bristow hid her moving lips behind a glass of sparkling champagne as she scanned the large ballroom, looking for her mark. Men and women milled about in their designer tuxedos and gowns, their laughter and congenial chatter crowding the air. A string quartet played a lilting, classical repertoire to heighten the elegance of the room, but at a low enough volume to keep from intruding on the conversations taking place among the elite guests. Everywhere Sydney looked there was another older man slipping his finger across the shoulder of another beautiful woman. A group of displaced-looking scientists debated in a corner as student waiters and waitresses slid noiselessly about, refilling glasses and offering hors d'oeuvres.

Holding court near the back of the room was the university president, graciously meeting guests and accepting their sizable donations for California University's science department. The party was in full swing, but there was still no sign of the host, a star biochemist and highly regarded member of the department, Dr. Lance Bergin, the man Sydney and her partners had come to see. And to take into custody.

"I didn't attend a single one of my birthday parties until I was fourteen years old," Eric Weiss said in Sydney's ear, even though they were separated by thirty yards and about a hundred people. The miracles of modern technology. Sydney had a speaker in her ear that was so tiny, even someone tucking her hair back for her wouldn't be able to see it. "I mostly just hid under the tablecloth in the dining room, sneaking cupcakes."

"That explains so much," Michael Vaughn said.

Sydney smirked and glanced in Vaughn's direction. He was standing just to the left of the bar in a tweed jacket and thick glasses, his hair mussed and his five o'clock shadow darkening his jaw. Even disheveled, he was still, in Sydney's opinion, the most handsome man in the room. Her eyes slid past him, barely making contact with his, and fell on the short, balding man in the too-tight waistcoat who had just stepped tentatively into the room. A taller man with glasses whispered something into his ear, then slipped away, leaving the balding man to greet his guests.

"Dr. Lance Bergin," Sydney whispered.

The doctor looked around nervously, clearly uncomfortable in the role of the host, then smiled obsequiously as an older man stepped forward to shake his hand. As they parted, both of them wiped their palms on their jackets. Turning away from Bergin, the older man grimaced in disgust as he moved on. Already busy greeting other guests, the balding man failed to notice. Working this guy was going to be a piece of cake.

"I'm going in," Sydney said, moving away from the wall.

"Let him schmooze a little more before you

swoop down on him," Vaughn said. "He may not be so easily seduced if he hasn't had some face time."

"Have you *seen* who you're talking to?" Weiss asked.

"Point taken," Vaughn replied.

Just then, Sydney stepped in front of a huge plate-glass window and caught a glimpse of her own reflection in the dark pane. A short, blond wig grazed her sharp cheekbones, highlighting her huge brown eyes. The glittery gold gown she wore clung to her curves and swished deliciously around her ankles, tickling them with every step. She looked, in a word, breathtaking. All just part of another day's work.

"This guy is never going to know what hit him," Weiss said with a laugh in his voice.

"In more ways than one," Sydney added under her breath.

Sydney sauntered toward Dr. Bergin, sizing him up as she approached. He had long, unkempt sideburns, and a patch of stubble on the underside of his chin he had missed during shaving. His paisley cummerbund was riding up a bit, exposing a line of his white shirt along its bottom hem. As various well-wishers approached and chatted with him,

Bergin barely met their eyes. It was difficult to believe that anyone this skittish and insecure could have had the confidence to create a bioweapon as dangerous as the one Bergin had reportedly concocted. According to intelligence reports, his VX411 was one of the deadliest compounds ever conceived. Unfortunately, the CIA had no idea how the VX411 was contracted, what its effects would be, or why Bergin had been compelled to create it in the first place. These were the facts Sydney and her team had been sent to uncover.

Sydney stepped up next to the evil scientist. He cleared his throat and looked up at her uncertainly. Sydney had at least four inches on him.

"Dr. Bergin, it is such an honor to finally meet you," Sydney said, extending her hand.

"Uh . . . yes . . . hell . . . hello," Dr. Bergin replied, touching her fingers quickly. Sydney refrained from wiping her hand. He had left a nice layer of sweat on her fingertips.

"My name is Cora Barlow," Sydney said, touching her hand to her chest. She filled her eyes with awe and went on as breathlessly as possible. "I read your paper in the *American Journal of Medicine*? The one about your recent breakthrough in a cure for Alzheimer's disease? And I just had to tell you in person how you've changed my life. My whole family's life, really."

Sydney slid her arm through Bergin's and turned him around, walking him toward the cavernous hallway beyond the lavishly set buffet table and away from the eager guests in the ballroom.

"It . . . it changed your life? How, exactly?" Bergin asked, clearing his throat again.

"Well, Grandpa Barlow, my father's father, was recently diagnosed with early stage Alzheimer's," Sydney said, tears springing to her eyes right on cue. "You know how it is when you learn that this disease has affected someone you love. It's just . . . devastating. Like a death sentence. Grandpa Barlow . . . he didn't get out of bed for days. He was so depressed." She paused near the entrance to the deserted hallway. "But your work, it brought us hope. Grandpa's back to his old self again. Just knowing that the possibility for a cure is out there . . . it brought him back."

Dr. Bergin flushed with pleasure. "Well . . . we're still years away from an actual *cure*. . . ."

"But to know that someone as brilliant as you is working on a solution . . . ," Sydney said.

Apparently overcome by emotion, Sydney brought her hand to her face. Dr. Bergin looked around, uncomfortable, and finally fumbled for the handkerchief in his pocket. He held it out to Sydney, and she took it with a grateful smile.

"Thank you so much," she said, touching the tiny cloth to her eyes. "You are so kind."

"Of . . . of course," Bergin said, glancing down the hallway. There was no one in sight, and not a soul had followed them out of the bustling ballroom. Still, it seemed as if Bergin was worried that someone would approach them at any moment. An odd fear, considering they were standing in Bergin's own home. What was he so scared of? Whatever it was, it was making it difficult for him to focus on Sydney, which was crucial to the task at hand.

"You know, I would love to see your laboratory," Sydney said, taking a step closer to Dr. Bergin. "See where you work. Where all your genius is put into practice."

Dr. Bergin flushed and looked around, backing himself into the wall. A rivulet of sweat trickled down one of his sideburns and clung to his chin. *Now* she had his full attention. It was almost too easy. She reached out and ran her fingertips along his lapel.

"Really?" Dr. Bergin squeaked.

"Oh, yes," Sydney replied with a small smile, moving even closer so that their bodies were nearly touching. She looked directly into his eyes, making it perfectly clear that she didn't just want to see his lab.

Dr. Bergin inhaled deeply. When he let it out, his breath smelled like mushrooms.

"Follow me," he said. "It's upstairs."

He slid away from her and scurried toward a wide staircase.

"Upstairs? Syd, our intel has the lab downstairs," Vaughn said in her ear. "In the basement."

Sydney couldn't exactly answer him without arousing Bergin's suspicions and she couldn't exactly tell Bergin that she knew he was going the wrong way in his own home, so she had to go along and play it from the hip. Bergin pushed open a big oak door and held it for Sydney. She stepped into a large, darkened library filled with heavy, scientific texts and half a dozen leather chairs.

"It's a little musty, for a lab," Sydney said lightly.

Bergin closed the door with a thump, blocking

out what little light they had. "I thought we would be more comfortable here," he said.

A small, green banker's lamp flicked on, and Sydney could now see the eager and somewhat nervous expression on Bergin's face. *How attractive,* Sydney thought sarcastically.

Sydney took a step toward him, knowing exactly how to play this game. "Sit down," she told him in her most commanding voice.

"Wh . . . what?" Dr. Bergin said.

Sydney reached out and pushed him, hard. Bergin fell back into the leather chair behind him, radiating excitement and anticipation. Sydney leaned over him and grew closer . . . closer . . . until he was practically drooling on her cleavage.

She suddenly grabbed his arms and pinned them to the chair.

"Hey! What's going on?"

"Where's the lab?" Sydney asked, tightening her grip.

Bergin struggled, but to no avail. He was unsurprisingly weak. "You don't have to be so rough," he whined.

"Yes, actually, I do," Sydney said. "My name is Sydney Bristow. I'm a government agent and I happen to know that you have a bioweapon hidden in the lab in your basement."

Bergin's watery eyes widened, and he slumped down in the chair. Sydney wasn't sure if this was a new tactic for escape or if she had just scared all the air right out of him. She had a feeling it was the latter.

"Now, you are going to take me down there and show me exactly where you're storing this stuff, or we are going directly to my boss, who, trust me, is a lot stronger, a lot less pretty, and a lot crueler than I am," Sydney said. That wasn't entirely true—at least not the "stronger" part—but it was all designed to intimidate the little weasel.

Dr. Bergin got the insinuation. He winced in pain as Sydney's grip tightened even further.

"All right! All right! I'll take you down there," he said, practically blubbering. "Just no torture, okay? I can't handle torture."

Shocker, Sydney thought, releasing his arms. Bergin rubbed his wrists, looking betrayed.

"Don't try to run or alert anyone. I'm not the only one here," Sydney told him as she stood up straight and smoothed her gown. "If you cooperate, I can make things a lot easier for you."

"Wh . . . what do you need, exactly?" Bergin asked, standing on unsteady legs.

"All the samples of the VX411 and its vaccine," Sydney said matter-of-factly. "There is a vaccine, I assume."

"Ye . . . yes," Bergin stammered.

Thank God, Sydney thought. A bioweapon with no antidote would be the absolute worst-case scenario. "And I'll be copying your computer files as well," she told him.

Bergin let out a strained whimper and walked past her toward the door, his shoulders hunched. Sydney knew his life was flashing before his eyes. Once she, Vaughn, and Weiss had collected all the evidence, Bergin was basically done for. Of course, considering what he had been up to, Sydney didn't really care. He was going to get exactly what he deserved.

Bergin led Sydney downstairs and back into the party. As they crossed the room, a few people stopped Bergin and commented on the lavish event or congratulated him on his latest grant. With each encounter, Bergin grew paler, sweatier, and more nervous, but no one seemed to notice. Luckily, this was Bergin's usual demeanor.

"And who's your lovely companion, Dr. Bergin?" a gentleman in an Armani tuxedo asked him, giving Sydney the once-over and clearly liking what he saw.

"Uh . . . she—"

"Cora Barlow," Sydney said, extending one hand and placing the other firmly on Bergin's arm. "Lance here is just taking me on a tour of his beautiful home."

"I'll bet," the man said with an appreciative nod. "I'll let you two get back to it."

"Thank you. It's been a pleasure," Sydney said, pulling Bergin away. "You're doing fine," Sydney said in Bergin's ear as he stumbled a bit on his way to the door at the far side of the room. "Just keep moving."

"Syd, there's a guy headed your way—more pro wrestler than scientist," Vaughn said in her ear. "Watch your back."

Adrenaline started to rush through Sydney's veins. She scanned her immediate surroundings as Bergin reached the door and opened it. The only potentially suspicious guy she saw was Weiss, who was nonchalantly following her as he chowed down on some shrimp scampi.

Bergin led Sydney into another hallway and

was about to close the door behind them when a beefy hand stopped it. The door was shoved open by a broad man with huge shoulders and a goatee. The seams of his tux looked fit to burst, and he puffed up his chest as he approached them. Dr. Bergin tripped backward so quickly, Sydney had to steady him with her hand.

What is going on around here? Sydney wondered.

"Good evening, Dr. Bergin," the man said in a gravelly voice. He glanced dismissively at Sydney. "Where are we going?"

"I . . . uh . . . I was just giving my friend Carla—"

"Cora," Sydney corrected.

"Right! Cora. I was just giving Cora here a tour of the house," Dr. Bergin replied, clasping his hands together.

"I don't think that's a wise idea, do you?" the man said.

"I just—"

Over the man's massive shoulders, Sydney saw Weiss slip into the hallway. She lifted her foot in its four-inch gold heel onto the upholstered bench next to her and bent down to refasten the buckle on the strap. The maneuver gave the hulk of a man a perfect view down her dress, which he enjoyed in earnest. In the split second he was distracted, Weiss grabbed a brass vase and slammed him over the back of the head with it. The wrestler's eyes rolled back into his head and he crumpled to the ground, slamming his temple against the wooden arm of the bench.

"That's gonna leave a mark," Weiss said.

"You guys, there's a couple more of them headed your way," Vaughn said. "Better get a move on."

"All right," Sydney said, racing down the hall and pulling Bergin with her. "Vaughn, do your thing."

Michael Vaughn yanked out the colorful flyers he had stashed in the back waistband of his pants and jumped up onto the bar. To get the crowd's attention, he kicked a few glasses and a bottle of hundred-dollar Scotch to the floor, where they smashed into bits and sprayed the nearest partygoers with sour brown liquid. A few gasps and screams let Vaughn know he had the floor to himself.

"This university supports Indonesian sweat-shops!" Vaughn shouted at the top of his lungs, raising his arms over his head. "All the clothing in the university bookstore is imported from third-world factories! Children as young as six years old working in squalor for pennies, just so students can wear propaganda! Stop the madness!"

He tossed out flyers to the nearest onlookers, most of whom let the pages flutter to the floor.

"Hey, buddy. What're you doing?" the young bartender asked, looking up at Vaughn nervously. "Get down from there before you get me fired."

"Don't you care about the plight of third-world laborers?" Vaughn shouted, his eyes wild.

"Actually, I kind of care about the plight of this laborer," the bartender hissed, glancing left and right. "I gotta make tuition."

From all corners of the room, Vaughn saw the rest of Bergin's guards scurrying toward him. The two guys he had noticed following after pro-wrestler man turned and headed straight for the bar. Vaughn hid a smile, knowing he had done his job. For the moment, Sydney and Weiss were safe to get on with the mission. Vaughn kept on shouting until the guards took him down.

"Down here," Bergin said, shoving through what seemed like the hundredth door in a row and clomping down a few cement steps. He turned down a slim hallway that trailed at least fifty feet before turning another corner.

"What do you have down here, a football stadium?" Weiss asked.

"I need a lot of space for my work," Bergin told him, approaching a metal door. "This is it."

Sydney glanced at the keypad next to the door. A red light blinked in warning. "Open it," she said, listening to the sounds of pounding feet coming from above. Vaughn had bought them some time, but she had no idea how much. "Open it now."

"Okay! Okay! Don't rush me!" Bergin said. His fingers trembled as he reached for the keypad.

Weiss looked toward the ceiling. "You sure have a lot of man power for a guy on a science professor's salary."

Bergin punched in a series of numbers and hit the large button at the bottom of the pad. "Well . . . you know . . . have to protect my . . . research . . . ," he mumbled.

The door buzzed and the lock clanged free just as another guard in a tuxedo slid around the corner. "Stop right there!" he shouted. He fired off a shot, and the bullet hit the wall and ricocheted down the hallway.

"Inside!" Sydney shouted, shoving Bergin through the door. Weiss fired one retaliatory round as he jumped in, closing the door safely behind them. Someone slammed into it the second it was shut.

"Anyone else know the code?" Sydney asked.

"No. No one," Bergin said, shaking his head.

"They'll find a way in," Weiss said as the pounding intensified. "Let's get this over with."

Sydney turned and found herself facing another door, this one made of heavy glass. The lab was just beyond—a white, antiseptic room with four long, chrome tables in the center. Along the walls were glass-fronted, climate-controlled storage cabinets, each filled with hundreds of vials and beakers. It was a good thing they had coerced Bergin into cooperating. It would have taken hours to search that room.

"You'll need to wear these," Bergin said, lifting a protective suit from a hook on the wall. He slid a huge helmet down from a shelf and started to dress himself. Meanwhile the pounding at the door intensified, accompanied by threats to Bergin to open up.

"I just love mad scientists," Weiss said sarcastically, putting his gun down and slipping into the blue coveralls.

Sydney secured her own gear, then zipped Weiss's hood to his suit. He did the same for her. Just when everything was snapped into place, the pounding stopped.

"Where are they going?" Sydney asked.

"I . . . I don't know," Bergin replied.

"Let's go," Weiss said, grabbing his gun.

The glass door let out a hiss of air as the hermetic seal was broken and Bergin led them into his laboratory.

"Weiss, the computer," Sydney said, nodding to the left. The computer station was set up along the nearest wall, the flat-screen monitor surrounded by piles and piles of disorganized papers.

"I'm on it," Weiss said. He quickly checked his protective gear for a place to stash his gun and, realizing there were no pockets in sight, he placed it on his lap as he slipped into the desk chair.

"All right, where's the VX411?" Sydney demanded.

Bergin pressed his lips together, wringing his hands in their plastic gloves. Sydney could see the beads of sweat forming along his hairline inside the mask. He was stalling, and Sydney didn't have time to humor him. She grabbed his arm and wrenched it behind his back, just enough to send a sharp, shooting pain all the way up his shoulder and into his skull.

"Tell me where it is right now, you twisted little psycho, or you're going to find out what I'm like when I'm angry," Sydney said through her teeth.

"You really don't want to do that, man," Weiss added, tapping away at the computer.

"Okay! Okay! Just let me go," Bergin shouted.

"Point me to the right cabinet," Sydney said.

"It's that one. Top left," Bergin told her, using his free arm to point.

Sydney let him go, and he cradled his elbow as he slid down onto the floor between two tables. She held her breath, her heart thumping in her ears as she opened the glass door on the cabinet. Inside were three grids filled with vials. Carefully, Sydney turned the labels on the first few bottles so that she could read them. There were a dozen samples of the VX411.

"Is this it?" Sydney asked.

"That's all. That's all I've got," Bergin gasped, still in pain.

Sydney glanced around and spotted a shelf of metal carrying cases. She pulled one down and opened the latch. The inside of the case was filled with thick foam, which had at least twenty vial-size cylinders cut out of it.

"What the hell?" Weiss said, staring intently at the computer screen.

"What is it?" Sydney asked.

"Some kind of security system I've never seen before. Bergin, get your ass over here," Weiss demanded.

The doctor looked from Weiss to Sydney and back again, clearly confused as to whose orders he should be following.

"Go!" Sydney told him.

As Bergin bent over Weiss's shoulder, looking pale and clammy and every bit like he was about to throw up into his protective helmet, Sydney focused on her own task. Ever so gently, she lifted the grid full of VX411 vials out of the refrigerated cabinet. The clear liquid swished and swirled inside the vials as she brought the metal grid to face level, and then placed it down on the counter-top next to the carrying case. Sydney stared at the poison, wondering just what horrors the world would suffer if this stuff got out of the lab.

Focus, she told herself. *You've got it now. Everything's going to be fine.*

With a steady hand, Sydney lifted the first vial of VX411 out of the grid and placed it carefully into one of the cylinders in the bag. It fit perfectly. Once the first vial was secure, Sydney worked more confidently, until finally the very last vial had been transferred. She had the weapon. Now all she needed was the antidote.

"Okay, where do you store the—"

Sydney looked up just in time to see Bergin grab something metal and shiny off a table and swing swiftly toward Weiss, a crazed look in his eyes.

"Weiss! Watch out!"

Eric spun around just as Bergin slashed down with what Sydney could now see was a tiny X-Acto knife. Weiss stopped Bergin's arm with his own, but not before the doctor made a nice clean slice in Weiss's protective gear, just along the neckline. Quickly, Sydney closed the case holding the VX411 and flipped the clasps closed. If there was going to be any kind of a scuffle, the most important thing was ensuring that the vials holding the deadly virus were safe—especially now that Weiss's gear had been compromised.

Weiss quickly subdued Bergin with a sharp jab to the stomach, and by the time Sydney came around the table, the doctor was cowering on the floor. She placed the case full of VX411 on the floor.

"I thought you were going to cooperate," Sydney said.

"I'm sorry! I'm sorry!" Bergin whined, holding his hands up to shield his face. "Please don't hurt me!"

Sydney rolled her eyes and looked at Weiss. "Did you upload all the files to Marshall?" she asked.

"Almost. I just have to—"

At that moment, Sydney and Weiss turned toward the front of the lab, their attention drawn by a loud, whirring noise. There was a sudden, deafening explosion, and the door burst free of its hinges in a whoosh of flames. Overhead, a piercing alarm sounded, drowning out Weiss's shouts and Bergin's cries. Two men wearing protective suits shoved their way into the lab, wielding guns.

Sydney looked around at the hundreds of vials filled with heaven knew what. Bullets and vials. This was not going to lead to anything good.

Weiss started furiously typing at the computer, uploading the rest of the files to Marshall as Sydney picked up the metal case and raced toward the door. If those men came in here, guns blazing, every vial in the place was going to shatter. She and Weiss had to get out of there as fast as possible.

The first intruder shoved through the lab's glass door and aimed at Sydney's head. "Don't move!" he shouted.

But Sydney didn't hesitate. She braced her left leg and executed a perfect kick to the man's face, bashing in the mask on his gear. It didn't shatter, but dented in far enough to break his nose. Blood gushed inside his helmet and the man screamed, flailing about. Cradling the case under one arm, Sydney grabbed his hand with her other hand and slammed it into the wall, releasing the gun. It fell to the floor and bounced away, sliding under a huge metal cabinet. Sydney was about to whirl around to face the other guard when he grabbed her from behind by her neck and pulled her up off her feet. Out of the corner of her eye, Sydney saw a third guard storm in. Weiss leaned down and grabbed his gun, which had fallen on the floor during the scuffle with Bergin.

"Don't shoot!" Sydney shouted at him. She knew he couldn't hear her over the blaring siren, but she hoped he would read her lips.

The grip around her neck tightened, and Sydney gently placed the metal case on the floor, then grabbed the man's beefy arm with both hands. Her legs kicked out, just barely missing a table filled with vials. Normally Sydney had no problem taking down a guy twice her size, but she felt like she was in a wrestling ring where the ropes were made of high-voltage electric wires. She had no room to maneuver and if she tried, she could break something lethal and Weiss could end up dead.

Sydney swung all of her weight to the right, forcing the man behind her to turn right as well. She reached back with both arms to grab his suit, crouched to the floor, and heaved the man over her head, flipping him into the only open space in the entire lab—the area by the door. She heard a loud crash behind her and knew Weiss had taken out one of the other guards. But what had they destroyed in the process? As Sydney turned she saw the computer smashed to bits against the wall and one of the bad guys lying unconscious in the debris. Weiss was taking on the fourth and final guard as Sydney noticed Bergin crawling toward the door.

"Where the hell do you think you're going?"

Sydney shouted, though she could hardly hear her own voice above the wailing alarm.

Bergin kept crawling and Sydney quickly picked up the case and lunged after him, but the guard she had laid out roused himself and grabbed her shoulder, yanking her back. Bergin jumped to his feet and ran through the smoldering door frame.

"Vaughn!" Sydney screamed into her comm as she fought off the guard. "Bergin's escaped. I repeat, Bergin's escaped! You have to go after him!"

She had no idea whether Vaughn heard her. In the next second the guard knocked the case from under her arm and sent it flying across the room. Sydney slammed a roundhouse kick into his gut, sending him careening into the glass wall. The impact was enough to knock him out, and he slid to the floor.

Sydney whirled around to check on the case. Her eyes widened in terror. The latch had popped open, and one of the vials was rolling toward the far wall. Sydney raced toward the fragile poisonous cylinder. If it broke, the VX411 would be released and then Weiss was a goner.

The vial rolled over and over as if in slow

motion. Sydney launched herself into the air to grab it and felt something catch her ankle. She glanced over her shoulder to find one of the guards reaching up from the floor, bringing her down.

"No!" she screamed, stretching her fingers toward the vial. It was just out of reach.

Sydney slammed into the floor, jarring every inch of her body, and watched the vial crack against the wall. Her stomach lurched as the clear liquid seeped out onto the floor, forming a small, innocuous-looking puddle.

Slowly, she turned to look at Weiss. He was just standing up after disarming his second guard. He saw the shattered vial, and the fear that covered his face was contagious. Sydney's eyes slowly trailed down to the gaping gash in his protective gear. Weiss looked as if he was about to faint.

The guard who had stopped her stood up, a wicked grin on his face as he hovered over Sydney.

You bastard, Sydney thought. *You idiotic bastard.*

She rolled over and, with every ounce of strength in her government-trained body, brought her right leg up swiftly and solidly into his groin.

CHAPTER 2

Weiss rifled through the beakers and bottles in a panic, checking every label in sight, looking for the VX411 vaccine. With each passing moment, his movements grew less sure—and more dangerous. Overhead, Bergin's useless siren continued to wail, a perfectly psychotic sound track for Sydney's current situation. Each rise and fall of the alarm raised her tension level higher.

"Weiss," Sydney shouted. Her own hands were working furiously, checking the vials on the first table. Any second, another troop of guards could burst in on them, making the task at hand even more difficult.

Weiss dropped a vial but grabbed it before it could roll off the table and smash on the floor. He put it back in its grid, took a deep breath, and kept searching. This was not good.

"Weiss!" Sydney shouted again. "You have to get out of here!"

Either ignoring her or unable to hear, Weiss turned from his table and started to search the next one. Sydney's heart pounded with trepidation and pity. He was fearing for his life. She knew he was trying to save himself. But if he kept this up, there was a good chance he was going to break something else and get exposed to yet another deadly virus.

"Weiss!" she tried again.

When he didn't acknowledge her this time, Sydney stopped what she was doing and crossed the room. She placed a hand on his back, gently, so that he wouldn't think he was under attack. "Eric!"

Finally, Weiss turned around, his chest heaving with each breath. His eyes were wide with terror.

"What?"

"You have to get out of here. You may not have even been exposed yet," Sydney told him.

"Are you kidding me? It's right there," Weiss said, gesturing toward the corner where the broken vial lay. "We have to find the antidote."

"We don't even know how this stuff is contracted," Sydney told him, doing her best to sound confident. "Maybe it's not inhaled. Maybe it has to be ingested or injected. We don't know."

"Yeah, sure. A massive bioweapon that has to be injected," Weiss said. "You don't believe that."

He was right. She didn't believe it. What she did believe was that every passing second was precious if they wanted to keep him from getting sick. Sydney looked Weiss in the eye and tried to radiate calm, even though a good part of her was also freaking out. Weiss was practically family.

"We will find the antidote," she said. "*I* will find the antidote. But for now, you have to get out of here before you get exposed to something else."

Weiss hesitated, looking toward the door.

"Come on, Eric, trust me," Sydney said. "I'll find it."

Even as she said the words she felt the hypocrisy of them. Here she was, asking Weiss to trust her when it was her own mistakes that had put him in this position in the first place. If only she had double-checked the latches on the case of VX411. If only she had kept an eye on Bergin. If only she hadn't left her back open so that guard could trip her up. If she had done her job, they wouldn't be in this mess.

"Weiss," Sydney said, taking control of her emotions. She had to focus. His life depended on it. Not to mention the object of their mission, which was at this point a much lesser, but still important, concern. "Weiss, go."

Eric cast her one last desperate look, then nodded and left the room, stepping over the prone bodies of the guards along the way. Sydney started where Weiss had left off, methodically checking each and every vial. She moved smoothly and swiftly along the long chrome table and found a complete set of bio-horrors along the way: strains of anthrax, smallpox, influenza, and other lesser-known, but seriously deadly diseases. It was all here. A perfect sampling of the worst that science had to offer. Sydney wished she had time to confiscate it all, but she had been sent in for the VX411 and its antidote, and that's what she was taking out of here. Arvin Sloane, the director of APO, could always send a team back later to sweep the entire mansion.

"Dammit," Sydney said under her breath, replacing the last vial in its grid. She glanced around the room. There were thousands more to look through, and any one of those guards could wake up at any moment. Then she would have to waste more of her precious time putting them down again. *What am I going to do?* she wondered, beginning to feel desperate.

Just keep going, she told herself, trying to ignore the incessant, ear-piercing wail of the siren. There wasn't much choice. She had to stay here until she found the vaccine, no matter how many goons she might have to fight off in the meantime.

Sydney was about to start on the next table when a laminated document attached to the wall caught her eye. It looked like a diagram of the lab. Sydney approached and saw that it was, in fact, a color-coded map with each cabinet's contents clearly marked. Sydney ripped the map from the wall. There was a whole area, marked in green, dedicated to vaccines.

Thank God, Sydney thought, racing toward

the first cabinet and yanking it open. Inside the door was another helpful list, cataloging the contents of each shelf. The VX411 vaccine was on the list. It was apparently sharing a grid with Bergin's latest attempts at a cure for Alzheimer's. Ironic, considering that was the disease that Sydney had used to get access to Bergin in the first place. How someone could be working so hard to cure something so awful, and at the same time be designing weapons that could kill millions, was beyond Sydney.

It didn't surprise her, however. In Sydney's line of work, she encountered psychotic criminals every day, and there was no telling what made most of them tick. But, it wasn't her job to figure them out. It was her job to stop them.

She turned to the cabinet and carefully lifted out the grid that the list indicated would hold the antidote. There were six vials filling up half the spaces. Sydney picked out the first and read the label.

VACCINE: ALZHEIMER'S, V. 2.12

She took a deep breath and replaced the bottle, lifting the next.

VACCINE: ALZHEIMER'S V. 3.05

Sydney gently replaced that vial, her pulse

starting to pound even harder. She checked the next vial and the next. They were all for Alzheimer's. Not a single label mentioned VX411. Quickly, Sydney pulled out the surrounding grids and checked them all, in case the vials she was looking for had been stashed in the wrong place. With each vial she checked, her panic level rose. The VX411 vaccine was not there.

Without the vaccine, and without Bergin, there was no way to save Weiss.

Why did you let Bergin get away? her mind screamed.

"Shotgun, this is Phoenix! Do you copy?" Sydney shouted into her comm.

At that exact moment the wailing sirens *finally* ceased, leaving an equally deafening ringing in her ears. The silence was disquieting. An eerie sense of doom settled over the lab.

"Go ahead, Phoenix," Vaughn responded, out of breath.

"Did you find Bergin?" she asked.

There was a pause, and Sydney said a little prayer. *Please don't let this mission be a failure. Please let Vaughn have Bergin. If he has Bergin, Weiss will be okay.*

"I checked everywhere, Phoenix," Vaughn said finally. "He's gone."

Sydney sat at her desk, which was situated in the center of the APO offices, and stared at the blinking cursor on her flat computer screen. Dressed in a black suit and a light blue shirt, her long brown hair hanging down her back, Sydney sat up straight and tried to concentrate. She was supposed to be working on her report concerning the Bergin mission, but she couldn't seem to begin. How was she supposed to put into words everything that had gone wrong?

But it wasn't just her guilt that was strangling her. Sydney's whole body was tense with anxiety, and she was completely on edge. Every movement in the office caught her attention. Every person she saw—Sloane, her father, Vaughn—she assumed was coming to tell her bad news—that Weiss was, in fact, infected. That he was going to die. That it was all her fault. She wished that she had her own office instead of a desk in the center of the open floor plan. APO's bright lights and glass partitions were torture in this situation. At the moment, she really needed a set of nice, solid walls to hide behind.

Come on, just do your work, Syd, she told herself. She placed her hands flat against the clear glass surface of her desk and pulled herself forward. *There's nothing you can do right now to change how the mission went.*

A huge part of Sydney's CIA training had involved learning to put mind over matter—to compartmentalize and shove aside the things that threatened to affect her or distract her. For years Sydney had been able to do that—to move on when an agent had died in the field, or when someone she knew went missing. She had even been able to put aside the more overarching dramas of her life—like her mother's supposed death when Sydney was just a child, and her father's inability to be there for her as a parent. She had rarely if ever let any of this affect her work. But for some reason, today, all her training was failing her.

The life of one of her best friends was at stake. He was downstairs in quarantine right now. There was no way she could compartmentalize that.

A door across the room from her opened and closed, and Sydney glanced up. This time it actually *was* Vaughn. She was hoping for a reassuring smile, but instead, his expression was grim and tight. Sydney's heart plummeted.

"What is it?" Sydney asked as Vaughn reached her desk.

Vaughn lifted the sides of his suit jacket and slid his hands into the pockets of his pants. He looked at the floor for a moment, gathering his composure, before meeting her gaze.

"They just confirmed the blood work," Vaughn said. "Weiss has contracted the virus."

"Oh, my God," Sydney said. All the oxygen was sucked right out of her. She had been expecting this, but it didn't make hearing the words any less awful. "Vaughn, I'm so sorry."

Her first instinct was to get up and hug him. Weiss was Vaughn's best friend, after all. They had known each other for years. Vaughn had to be terrified at the thought of losing Weiss. But something held Sydney to her chair: a determination that this news would come to mean nothing. She refused to give in to her emotions right now. They were going to save Eric. They had to.

"They're testing the samples of the virus that you recovered to see if we have anything that might work as a vaccine," Vaughn said. "They don't think they have time to start from scratch."

"Has he presented any symptoms?" Sydney asked.

"No," Vaughn said. "But since this is a new compound, we have no idea what the symptoms might be. We don't even know the gestation period. Weiss could die at any moment without even so much as sneezing. We just don't know."

At hearing this news, Sydney didn't hesitate. She got up and hugged Vaughn tightly, wishing she could squeeze the misery right out of him. As he wrapped his arms around her, the lump of guilt that had formed in her chest threatened to explode. All around the brightly lit APO offices, people went about their business, filing, talking, clicking away at their computers. Phones rang. Somewhere nearby, someone laughed. It all seemed so wrong. The world should have stopped by now.

"This is my fault," Sydney said quietly, miserably. "He's down there because of me."

Vaughn released her and looked into her eyes. He smoothed her hair with the palm of his hand. "What are you talking about?"

"The more I think about it, the more I recognize all the things I could have done differently,"

Sydney told him, shaking her head. "I should never have taken my eyes off Bergin. I should have made sure that guard was unconscious. I didn't secure the vials properly. I just—"

"Sydney, you know that what you're saying is insane," Vaughn told her. "We're all at risk on every one of our missions. There's no way to predict what might go wrong, and there's no way to prevent the unexpected."

"I know, but there *is* a way to prevent sloppiness," Sydney said.

Vaughn smiled slightly. "I've worked with you for four years and I've never known you to be sloppy."

Sydney took a deep breath. Vaughn could say whatever he wanted, but it didn't erase the truth. It didn't change the fact that Sydney was going to be replaying this mission in her mind for days, weeks, maybe even years to come.

"Does he know yet?" Sydney asked. "Does Eric know?"

Vaughn shook his head. "I was just on my way down there to break the news."

"I'm coming with you," Sydney said.

"You sure?" Vaughn asked.

"I'm sure," she replied. *I should go. I should*

be the one to have to tell him. "I want to be there."

Vaughn nodded, and together they headed for the elevators.

The silence was suffocating. Once Sydney finished relating the horrible news to Weiss, none of them seemed to be able to decide what to say next. Weiss pulled the metal chair over from the desk next to the wall and set it to face Sydney and Vaughn. He sat down heavily and let out a sigh. His very frame seemed to collapse, and he slumped forward. His forehead pressed against the thick glass that separated him from Sydney and Vaughn, his skin leaving a waxy print on the otherwise spotless surface.

"Well," he said finally, staring at the floor. "Well . . . there you go."

"Eric, listen, we're going to find that vaccine," Vaughn said firmly. "Bergin isn't some well-connected international terrorist mastermind. He's a local science professor. He can't be that hard to track. Marshall's working on the computer files you sent him right now."

"And you know that if anyone can find what we need, Marshall can," Sydney said.

Marshall was APO's resident technical mastermind. He could get the agents past any security system in the world and designed the high-tech gear for all their missions. He had executed hundreds and hundreds of missions and had never failed Sydney once in the five-plus years she had been working with him.

"Well, at least the guys in lab coats won't have to infect any mice with this stuff," Weiss joked lamely. "I got your guinea pig right here."

"Weiss," Vaughn said.

"What? Humor is my defense mechanism," Weiss shot back. "If you don't know that by now, you're not much of an agent."

Sydney smirked sadly and looked down at her square-toed shoes. Weiss may have been making light of the situation, but the doom in his eyes was unmistakable. They all knew that without Bergin's vaccine, he didn't stand a chance.

"Hey, don't look so down, you guys," Weiss said, standing again. "I needed a vacation."

Sydney and Vaughn exchanged a worried look just as the door behind them opened. Sydney's younger half sister, Nadia, an agent with APO and the object of the biggest crush of Eric Weiss's life, walked in, her heeled boots clicking along the high-gloss floor. Her brown hair was pulled back in a low ponytail, and her angular face was all business. She glanced reassuringly at Sydney and Vaughn before addressing Weiss.

"How are you doing?" she asked him, stepping up to the glass.

"About a thousand times better now," Weiss said with a wan smile.

Nadia smiled back. "My father has called a meeting in his office," she said, referring to Sloane. "Jack and Dixon are already there."

Sydney and Nadia shared the same mother, but different fathers—a fact for which Sydney thanked her lucky stars. It was difficult for her to accept that her mother had cheated on her father with a man like Arvin Sloane—she had a hard time even being in the same *room* with the man. There was no way she could survive if she shared Sloane's genes. Sydney had her issues with Jack Bristow, but Sloane was about a thousand times worse. Sometimes she had no idea how Nadia lived with the reality that she and Sloane were related by blood, except for the fact that Nadia had grown up in an orphanage and had just met her father last year. She hadn't been around for most of Sloane's crimes, and being an orphan who wanted nothing more than to know her family made it a lot easier to ignore the evidence of her father's vileness.

"I'm sure Marshall is on his way to finding something that will help," Nadia said, looking Weiss in the eye. "Everything's going to be fine."

Eric nodded and swallowed hard. Sydney hated seeing him locked in that tiny room. However comfortable the doctors tried to make it, it still seemed like a prison cell. And Weiss was waiting on death row.

"You should get some rest," Nadia told him, glancing at the twin-size bed in the corner of the square room.

"Yeah, like that's gonna happen," Weiss said.

For a long moment, they all just stood there, not looking at one another. All Sydney could see was the thick glass that separated herself, Vaughn, and Nadia from their friend. Sydney was overwhelmed by everything that glass represented. What she wouldn't give to be able to shatter it—to grab Weiss and pull him out of there and make everything go back to normal.

"Well, what are you guys just standing here

for?" Weiss said finally. "Get out there and save my fat ass already."

Nadia let out a small laugh and pressed her palm to the glass briefly before turning and heading back to work.

"We'll see you soon, man," Vaughn said.

Weiss nodded hopefully and Sydney cast him one last encouraging look before turning down the hall and leaving him behind. On their way out, they passed a team of medical technicians in protective suits, wheeling in a heart monitor and IV rigs and other machinery. No doubt they were going to hook Weiss up to every machine possible so that they could watch his vitals for any sudden changes. As the door closed behind Sydney, she glanced over her shoulder. Weiss stood helplessly inside his glass cell as the techs set up their equipment. He had never looked so small.

CHAPTER 3

Sydney was the last to enter the office of the APO director and she walked in feeling conspicuous. All eyes were trained on her. The paperwork had not been filed, but everyone knew what had happened on that mission. It was supposed to be routine. Bergin was supposed to be an easy mark. But Sydney had let things get out of hand. She had let Weiss down. She had let them all down.

I'm just going to have to make things right, Sydney told herself. *I have to find that vaccine.*

She sat down on one of the straight-backed red

couches that stood in a semicircle in front of Sloane's large desk and opened the black leather folder she had found at her own workstation. Glancing across the way, she nodded at Marcus Dixon, then caught her father's eye. Jack Bristow was known for his impeccable appearance and his impenetrable stare. Never a gray hair out of place unless he was in the field and his alias required it. Never a thread hanging from the sleeve of his perfect suits. Never an emotion betrayed. Today, however, he managed a tight, reassuring smile for his daughter as she joined the proceedings. Sydney wasn't sure if she should feel flattered that he made the effort, or chagrined because his trying to comfort her meant she really *had* messed up. As Vaughn, Marshall, and Nadia settled in around her, she averted her gaze and turned her attention to the large desk in front of her and the man sitting behind it.

A short and wiry man with dark gray hair and a close-cropped beard, Arvin Sloane commanded attention whenever he walked into a room. Even with his beady eyes and round glasses, he exuded power. Most people felt compelled to listen whenever he had something to say. Sydney, for the most part, just felt revulsion.

What had the CIA been thinking when they hired pure evil to run such an elite force as APO? Sydney felt that this was something she would never understand. Apparently, the United States government had decided that Sloane had reformed his sinister ways. Sydney was laboring under no such delusion. She knew what Sloane was, and she was just waiting for him to show the rest of the world his true colors. She was practically salivating for the day he would slip up and she would be able to take him into custody herself.

For now, however, he was her superior, and she had to pay attention to whatever he had to say. But she didn't have to like it.

"As you all know, our colleague and friend, Eric Weiss, has contracted a very deadly virus, Dr. Lance Bergin's own creation, VX411," Sloane began, getting up from his chair and walking around to the front of his desk.

Sydney cringed inwardly when Sloane named Eric as his "friend." He had no right to call anyone his friend, least of all a man with as big a heart as Eric Weiss had.

"The lab has done its tests on the vials of VX411 that Sydney retrieved," Sloane continued. He picked up a leather folder from the desk behind him and opened it, quickly scanning its contents. The rest of the team did the same. "They have discovered that VX411 is in fact a hybrid of two deadly toxins—the very well known and documented anthrax bacterium, and the lesser known but much more insidious Panther virus."

"Well, that's great!" Vaughn blurted.

A few eyebrows raised in surprise.

"How so, Agent Vaughn?" Jack Bristow asked.

"We have cures for both anthrax and the Panther virus," Vaughn said, sitting forward and closing his file. Sydney could practically feel the relief radiating from him. "Can't we just administer those vaccines?"

"Actually, the doctors are treating Agent Weiss with those vaccines even as we speak," Marshall said, looking up from the screen on his tiny laptop. "But they don't think it's going to work. At least, not as a cure. It might delay the symptoms for a while, but we're still looking at something, well, bad. Very bad."

Sydney held her breath. "What exactly are the symptoms?"

"According to our current hypothesis, it's not

pretty," Sloane said, his tone flat. He put the folder down and crossed his arms over his chest tightly. "Once the VX411 has been inhaled or ingested, it presents itself within twenty-four hours as a severe flu. Meanwhile, the virus slowly breaks down the delicate lining of the stomach and the lungs, allowing fluid to fill the airways and the intestines and basically drown the victim from the inside out. It would be a slow and painful process, and within a few days, the victim will die."

Sydney looked at Vaughn. His face, like her own, had gone pale. Weiss did not deserve to die such a horrible death. *Nobody* deserved to die like that.

"We have to find that vaccine," Sydney said.

"I agree, Agent Bristow," Sloane said. "And as quickly as possible."

Sydney shifted in her seat. Sloane never called her "Agent Bristow," even in formal situations, unless he was angry at her. To him, it was a scolding, like when parents used their kids' middle names.

He thinks I'm responsible for this, she realized. For once in her life, she and Sloane were on the same page.

"Marshall, what did you get from Bergin's hard drive?" Sloane asked, lifting his chin slightly and looking down his nose at Marshall in that imperial way of his.

Marshall sat forward quickly, fumbled with his laptop, and cried out as it slipped from his hands and bounced once on the floor before landing at Sloane's feet. Muttering a few innocent epithets, Marshall dove for the computer, but slammed the back of his head on the corner of Sloane's desk as he came up. Papers and pens jumped and Marshall clutched the back of his head, holding the computer with his other hand.

"Are you all right?" Dixon asked, leaning over.

"Yeah, fine. Sorry, fine," Marshall said, standing up straight. He lifted the computer and smiled. "Titanium," he said. "Too bad my head isn't . . . ow." He winced as he touched the back of his skull. "Sorry. I've been up for twenty-four hours what with the kid being sick and then these files to decrypt and you know when you're tired and your spatial relations just go to hell?" He looked at them all and smiled ingratiatingly. Sydney tried to smile back, but her thoughts were too strained.

"Marshall," Sloane said in a warning tone.

"Right. Sorry. The hard drive," Marshall said. He sat down again and opened the laptop. Sydney could see dozens of files open on his screen. "Well, we're still decrypting some of the data. He's got one heck of a security system on there, so it'll be a little longer before we have the names of his money men. But we did find out that he rents a storage space just off campus, and it looks like he's got a bunch of stuff stashed there. Including some more samples of VX411 and its vaccine."

Sydney's heart leaped. A storage facility just off campus? That was less than an hour away! They could have the vaccine to Weiss in no time.

"The storage facility is at the center of a warehouse district," Sloane said, turning to the six flat screens on the east wall of his office. He hit a button on a tiny remote and a satellite photograph of the warehouse district appeared on all six screens. One of the long, low buildings had been colored red. "Security is at a minimum, so this should be a simple smash-and-grab operation. Still, we will be taking all the usual precautions. We can't afford any more mistakes."

Sydney glanced at Vaughn and Dixon. Somehow it felt like every word out of Sloane's mouth today was an admonishment directed at her.

"Sydney, Nadia, you will infiltrate the warehouse and gather all samples of both the VX411 virus and its vaccine," Sloane continued, looking at each of his agents. He walked around his desk again and stood behind it, pressing his fingertips into the surface. "We cannot let Bergin retain any samples of this virus. If this hybrid falls into the wrong hands and gets released into the food or water supply or even into an air duct at an office building, we will have a major disaster on our hands."

Sydney and Nadia both nodded. It was all Sydney could do to keep from jumping up from the couch right then. They had to get moving. Weiss was depending on them. With any luck, by tonight, this would all be just a bad memory.

"Dixon, you'll be leading another team back into Bergin's mansion," Sloane added. "I want that place searched completely. If a single vial of VX411 or the antidote was overlooked, I want it found."

"Yes sir," Dixon replied.

"All right, everyone," Sloane said as everyone stood. "Let's save Agent Weiss."

* * *

Sydney and Nadia crouched near the rusty wall of the warehouse diagonally across from Bergin's storage facility. Peering around the corner, Nadia held a pair of mini binoculars to her eyes and sighed before slipping back into hiding.

"These two look like a couple of amateurs," she said.

"You sound disappointed," Sydney replied, slipping her tranquilizer gun into the back waistband of her jeans. Her pulse was pounding in her ears. In less than ten minutes they would have the antidote to save Weiss. Her salvation was just a hundred yards and two inexperienced henchmen away.

"It just doesn't make sense," Nadia replied. "Why have all those experts at the mansion but assign these substandards here?" She glanced around the corner again. "If the key to Bergin's masterpiece is inside those walls, why not have the place locked down?"

"What can I tell you? The guy's new to the game," Sydney said. She adjusted her backpack on her shoulders and flipped one of her braids so that it hung down in front of her. "All right. Remember, one at a time."

"Got it," Nadia replied. "I would say be careful, but I'm not worried," she added with a smile.

Sydney smiled back, then stood and strolled out from their hiding place. She looked around at the walls of the warehouses, appeared confused, and gripped the straps on her backpack. Turning in a small circle, Sydney bit her lip and feigned distress. Finally, her eyes lit on the two men standing outside Bergin's warehouse and her face brightened. She flashed her sweetest smile.

The men were both potbellied and middle-aged, wearing flannel shirts and jeans. They looked more like construction workers than highly paid security guards, but it was clear they were both armed. The taller of the two had a conspicuous bulge at the side of his shirt, near his hip. The other one noticed Sydney approaching and slid his own piece from the front of his waistband around to the back.

Nadia's right, these two are total rookies, Sydney thought.

"Excuse me! Do you know where Bennington Hall is?" Sydney asked, pitching her voice up an octave and putting on a thick Southern accent. She jutted out one hip and held a hand over her eyes, blocking the sun.

"No. And you shouldn't be here, girlie," the taller man said.

Sydney slumped her shoulders and looked around again. "I don't understand. Those guys told me to make a right on McCormack and I couldn't miss it. But I ended up here. What part of campus *is* this?"

The two guys exchanged a look and grinned maliciously. "Honey, you ain't on campus anymore," the shorter one said. "I think those guys were just having some fun with you."

"What? *No!* I have to get to Bennington Hall!" Sydney said, starting to tear up. "I have my first French class today and I can't start out on the wrong foot. I could lose my scholarship and then I'll have to go back to Louisiana and my uncle Jimmy and I . . . just . . . can't—"

"Whoa, whoa, whoa. Calm down," the taller man said, holding his hands up.

"Do you have a map around here anywhere?" Sydney asked, sniffling. "I mean, I must be close."

The men exchanged another glance, and finally the shorter, stockier one turned toward the warehouse door. "Maybe we got something in the office," he said. "Lemme just go check."

"Thank you. Thank you *so* much," Sydney said, clasping her hands together.

The moment he closed the door behind him, an orange tranquilizer dart hit the taller man right in the neck. His eyes went wide, and he grasped the wound for a split second before falling to the ground. Sydney squared herself next to the door and waited. It opened with a creak, and the other man walked out, his eyes trained down on a wrinkled map.

"All right, this one's kinda outdated, but I think we can find your class," he said.

He never saw the dart coming. His prone partner and his fat gut cushioned his fall as the map fluttered to the ground. Nadia was one heck of a good shot.

Nadia raced over and helped Sydney drag the unconscious bodies into the warehouse, in case anyone happened to come by. They laid the men next to a rickety, glass-walled office and closed the door behind them.

"We're in," Sydney said into her comm.

Now all they had to do was find the vaccine and destroy the VX411.

* * *

Marcus Dixon was on his guard, gun drawn as he crossed the eerily silent ballroom at Lance Bergin's opulent hillside mansion. Even in the middle of the day, the room was filled with dark shadows. Thick velvet curtains had been drawn over the tall windows, all but extinguishing the sunlight. Behind him, a team of six men and women followed, toting equipment for gathering the rest of Bergin's samples. Dixon approached the doors to the hallway that, according to Sydney's instructions, would eventually lead to Bergin's lab. He kicked the door open and pointed his gun into the empty corridor, but even as he followed these basic procedures, he knew it was unnecessary. This place felt more deserted than a tomb.

"All clear," he said into his comm, glancing down the pitch-black hallway.

Just let there be something in that lab that Sydney missed, he thought as he led the team along the plush carpeted floor. *Let me find something to help Weiss. . . .*

"Are you sure you should be standing, man?" Vaughn asked Weiss as he stepped into his friend's tiny room.

Weiss had changed into a pair of black sweats and an oversize heather gray T-shirt. A bag from a fast-food place was crumpled in the garbage, and a stack of DVDs that Marshall had brought him lay on the table next to the bed. Aside from the wires and tubes he was hooked up to, he looked like a guy who was on vacation.

"Are you sure you want to be in the same room with me?" Weiss asked. He smiled, but his eyes told a different story. He was feeling scared and sorry for himself. Vaughn was here to try to distract him.

"Well, the doctors say the virus can't be transmitted from one person to another without exchange of fluid," Vaughn replied. "So as long as you're not planning on slipping me the tongue . . ."

"Just get me out of these wires and I'm all yours," Weiss joked, lifting his arm.

Vaughn smirked and tried not to stare at the monitors. Tiny white wires ran out the sleeves and neck of Weiss's shirt, attached to various computers in the corner. A pair of small, round pads had been glued to Weiss's temples and these were also hooked up to a monitor, making it difficult for Weiss to move around freely. Each of the sensors was monitoring another of Weiss's vitals—his heart rate, his temperature, his brain waves—all searching for that tiny blip, that small abnormality that would signal the first trace of the virus.

"Anyway, I figure I may as well stand now, while I can," Weiss said, pacing a little, causing the long wires to stretch to their limits. "From the sound of things, I may not be able to do it for much longer."

Vaughn swallowed back a lump that was beginning to form in his throat. *Don't let him go there,* he thought. *Don't let* yourself *go there.* Vaughn knew that if he allowed himself to dwell on the reality of what was happening to his friend, he would not be able to do Weiss any good.

"Unbelievable," he said lightly. "I never thought I'd see the day when the country's number one couch potato actually wanted to stand."

"I know, right?" Weiss said, touching the top of one of the monitors.

He fiddled with an IV in the corner and ran his hand along the top of the desk. Vaughn's heart broke as he watched his friend trying to hold on to everything he could. It was a classic symptom of a terminal patient. They tried to touch things, grasp things, subconsciously thinking that if they could grab on to something solid, they could anchor themselves in the present. With every touch, Weiss's movements were shakier—more manic. Vaughn had to calm him down. Getting worked up was not going to help his condition.

"Hey, remember that time when we got New Year's week off?" Vaughn asked, sliding his hands into his pockets.

"Are you kidding? That was one of the best weeks of my life," Weiss said with a smile.

"Ten bowl games over four days and you never once moved off that couch," Vaughn said, chuckling.

"Excuse me, I did occasionally use the bathroom," Weiss reminded him. "And someone had to get up to answer the door for the pizza guy."

"Yeah, and I believe that someone was me," Vaughn said. "I think you still owe me the hundred bucks I shelled out to all the fast-food places in town."

"Oh, come on! I totally paid you back!" Weiss exclaimed, moving away from the wall.

"You did not! Wait, you're not still counting that poker game," Vaughn said with a laugh. This was working. Weiss was, at least for the moment, focusing on something other than his health.

"I let you win!" Weiss protested.

"I had a full house! Queens over tens!" Vaughn said. "There's no way you had a hand to beat that."

"Four fives, baby," Weiss said, rubbing his hands together gleefully. "I am the poker master."

Vaughn's jaw dropped. "You did not have four fives! I know for a fact that you did not have four fives."

"Yes, I did! I can't believe you're still trying to argue this after all this time!" Weiss said, puffing his chest out and opening his arms. "I . . . let . . . you . . . you . . ."

Vaughn's heart gave a sudden lurch as he watched all the color drain from Weiss's face. Droplets of sweat appeared along his hairline in a matter of seconds.

"Weiss?" Vaughn said, stepping forward.

"You . . . win," Weiss said weakly.

And then his eyes rolled back into his head and he collapsed forward, right into Vaughn's waiting arms.

"Weiss! Weiss!" Vaughn shouted as the monitors went wild. He strained to support the dead weight in his arms. "Hey! I need some help in here! Somebody get in here!"

Within seconds, two medics raced into the room and started shouting questions at Vaughn. He answered them as best he could while helping them lift his friend onto the bed in the corner.

"Agent Vaughn, you'll have to leave the room while we tend to Agent Weiss," one of them told Vaughn, some guy Vaughn knew he had met but couldn't remotely place in all the panic. "Vaughn," the medic said, steering him toward the door firmly. "We'll take care of him. Don't worry."

Vaughn felt his head nodding as he stepped out of the room. The second the door closed behind him, he snapped to. They needed to find that vaccine. Weiss was clearly in serious danger. His heart felt like it was pounding inside his skull as he grabbed the phone on the wall and hit Marshall's extension.

"Marshall," he barked into the phone. "Have you heard from Syd and Dixon?"

"Agent Vaughn," Marshall sounded surprised by his panicked tone. "Uh, no. They haven't checked in yet."

"Patch me through to Sydney," Vaughn said,

trying not to watch as the medics pressed a needle into Weiss's arm on the other side of the glass.

"I don't think—"

"Just do it, Marshall," Vaughn demanded.

He rested his forehead against the cool brick wall and squeezed his eyes shut. *I may never speak to Eric again,* he thought. *I may never see him again.*

"Vaughn! What's going on?" Sydney whispered.

"Syd, Weiss is getting sick," Vaughn said, gripping the phone as if he could somehow hold on to her. He felt like he was holding on for dear life. "He just faded dead away right in front of me. Tell me you have the vaccine."

"Don't worry, Vaughn," Sydney said calmly. "We're in."

"Did you hear that?" Sydney asked Nadia.

"Weiss is in trouble," Nadia said with a curt nod.

As silently as possible, they ascended the set of metal stairs that climbed up above the warehouse's office and led to the one and only door in the place. No matter how lightly she stepped, Sydney's heavy boots caused reverberations that sounded to her as loud as a bomb blast. The guards outside may have been taken care of, but there could still be people waiting on the other side of that door. Lab technicians, researchers, more guards, maybe even Bergin himself. The last thing Sydney wanted to do was alert them to her presence. Things had gone horribly awry the last time that had happened.

Nadia arrived at the platform at the top of the steps and stood to one side of the metal door. Sydney pressed herself back against the opposite wall and nodded at her sister.

This is it, Sydney told herself. *Whatever or whoever is behind this door is all that stands between Weiss and a cure.*

She held her breath, reached for the handle, and yanked the door open. Nadia slipped through, drawing her gun, and Sydney quickly followed. They were standing on a long catwalk with another set of descending stairs at the end, looking out over a huge warehouse. As Sydney approached the guardrail, Nadia's arms fell down at her sides. Somehow, Sydney knew she didn't want to look over, but she did.

There was nothing. Nothing but a couple of

overturned tables and row upon row of empty shelves. A computer station had clearly been ripped from the wall, and the desk it had been sitting on had been picked clean. Packing material littered the concrete floor, and a forklift stood idle in the corner.

Whatever Bergin had stored here, it was gone. Sydney felt as if her insides had been hollowed out as well.

"Marshall, patch me through to Dixon," Sydney said, turning away from Nadia. There was no way she could look anyone in the eye just now.

"You're through," Marshall said in her ear.

"Dixon, what've you got?" Sydney asked, hoping against hope that she had, in fact, missed something on her last sweep of the lab.

"We got nothing, Syd," Dixon replied. "Someone's cleared the whole place out. There's not so much as a test tube left."

Sydney's heart dropped like the empty, spent shell of a bullet. She leaned into the guardrail and gasped for breath.

"What about you?" Dixon asked. There was a pause as Sydney tried to calm herself. "Sydney? Nadia?"

Nadia placed her hand on Sydney's back and replied. "Same here, Dixon. The place is empty."

He got rid of everything, Sydney thought, her mind whirling. *We have nothing. No cure. No leads.*

He may have been new to the game, but Bergin had done a thorough job of covering his ass, and now Weiss's life was as good as over.

CHAPTER 4

Sydney took a deep breath and tried to quell the dread in her heart as she stepped up to the glass wall of Weiss's room. Vaughn had warned her that, although Weiss was officially listed in stable condition, he wasn't doing well. Sydney had accordingly prepared herself for the worst. But seeing him there, lying back against the pillows of his hospital bed with his eyes closed, she was hit with an iron fist to the chest. He looked so pale, so small. She could almost imagine what he had looked like as a child. The thought brought home the reality of how close he was to death. In a couple of days, Weiss could be gone, and his death would be on Sydney's shoulders.

Stop feeling sorry for yourself, Sydney thought, straightening up. *You're here for Weiss.*

She reached for the door and put on her brightest smile. As she approached the bed, Sydney expected Weiss to open his eyes and turn to find out who had come to visit, but he didn't move a muscle. Her smile started to fade. His chest didn't appear to be moving.

"Oh, my God, Weiss? Weiss!" Sydney reached out and touched his arm. It was burning hot. Much better than freezing cold, but still disturbing. He had to be running a dangerously high fever.

"Weiss, wake up," Sydney said. She knew he needed his rest, but she had to see that he was okay. Slowly, Weiss's eyes fluttered open.

Thank God, Sydney thought, letting out a breath of relief. It wasn't until that moment that she heard the heart monitor beeping away and all the other machines whirring, confirming that Weiss was still with her. She should have noticed the monitors, but in her panic, she had blocked them out.

Way to stay cool under pressure, she chided herself.

"Hey," Sydney said with a smile as Weiss finally focused in on her.

"Hey." His voice was raspy, and he started to cough. He brought his hand to his mouth as his whole body shook.

Sydney grabbed the plastic pitcher of water next to his bed and quickly poured him a cupful. Weiss downed it all in one gulp.

"Thanks," he said, leaning back with the empty cup against his chest. "I'm a little dehydrated."

"And a little hot," Sydney added. "Do you want some ice? They have a whole bucket over here."

"Sure," Weiss said with a small nod.

Sydney dug another plastic cup into the ice bucket and handed it to Weiss. She pulled up a chair and sat down at his side as he crunched on the small cubes. It seemed like it was taking him a lot of effort. For the first time Sydney noticed the dark purple circles under his eyes.

"Do you want me to go?" Sydney asked. "Let you get some more sleep?"

"No!" Weiss blurted, causing Sydney's eyes to

widen. "Sorry. No," he said in a more normal tone of voice. "I know it's cliché, but I'm kind of trying to avoid sleep as much as possible. You know . . . scared I won't wake up again."

Sydney ignored the hot sting behind her eyes and smiled. "That's not gonna happen," she said.

"It may happen," Weiss said.

"We won't let it," Sydney replied, trying to feel as confident as her words sounded. "Come on, when have you ever known me and Vaughn to fail on a mission?"

"Well, let's see . . . he was married to the enemy, and you did sort of disappear on us for a couple of years . . . ," Weiss joked. "That kind of behavior doesn't exactly instill confidence."

"At least you still have your sense of humor," Sydney said with a grin.

"Yeah, well," Weiss said. He sighed and placed another ice cube in his mouth. "Really, though," he said, trying to meet her eye, "how's it going? I mean, I assume you haven't found the antidote yet, or some doctor on a white horse would have ridden in here and hit me with a needle already."

Sydney leaned forward and looked at the floor. Part of her felt that Weiss should know about the failed attempts at the warehouse and at Bergin's mansion—that he deserved to know the truth about his situation. But it was only a very small part of the big picture. Sometimes the truth can be detrimental, and she knew this was one of those times. If Weiss knew that the team had gotten basically nowhere, it would cause him serious stress, and his body didn't need that right now. He had to stay positive.

"No, we don't have it yet," Sydney said finally. "But we will. Every APO agent in the office is working on it. You met Bergin. He's no match for us."

"Oh yeah, I met Bergin," Weiss said. "Weasel tried to slit my throat with an X-Acto knife."

"Yeah, but he didn't," Sydney reminded him. "You lived to see another day."

The moment the words were out of her mouth, Sydney wanted to take them back. Weiss may have lived one more day, but how many more did he actually have? She watched his face darken as the very same thought occurred to him. The growing sense of fear in the room was palpable.

Suddenly Sydney felt so trapped and useless, she wanted to punch something, or throw one of those stupid beeping machines at a wall. It wasn't

fair that Weiss had to go through this. There had to
be something she could do.

Sydney strode through the bullpen of the APO
offices, fueled by frustration. There was so much
pent-up energy inside of her, she felt like she
could run a marathon or go nine rounds with a
heavyweight. She had to be proactive. She had to
tackle this problem head-on. If she couldn't find
a way to be useful, she was going to go insane
with worry and guilt. Unfortunately, it was all up
to the computers now. If APO was going to get a
lead on Bergin and find out where he may have
stashed the vaccine, the lead was going to come
from his hard drive. Sydney had to go directly to
the source.

Marshall was so startled when Sydney came
barreling into his office, he nearly fell off his chair.
Hot coffee sloshed over the rim of his mug and
splattered onto the leg of his pants.

"Man, that's hot!" Marshall exclaimed, jumping up. He placed the mug on his chrome-topped
desk, spilling even more, and grabbed a napkin to
dab at his pants. Bent over at the waist, he looked
up at Sydney and slowly stopped dabbing.

"Hey, Syd," he said, eyeing her warily. "Everything okay?"

"Where are we with the Bergin files?" Sydney asked, crossing her arms over her chest.

"Oh, well, you wouldn't believe the encryption program this guy has," Marshall said, excited. He crumpled up the napkin and tossed it toward his overflowing garbage can, missing it by three feet. "I've never seen anything like it before, and you know I've seen pretty much everything. I'd love to meet the guy . . . or girl, of course . . . who designed this. I mean it's just—"

"I get it. It's genius," Sydney said flatly. "How long till you crack it?"

Marshall's face fell. He smoothed his tie and sat down again, pulling his chair toward his workstation. "It's gonna be another couple of hours, at least," he said with an apologetic grimace. "I've got Bernie running the code through the—"

"Two hours?" Sydney snapped. "Marshall, we don't have that kind of time!"

The door behind Sydney opened, and Nadia slipped into the room noiselessly. She looked from Marshall's nauseous expression to Sydney's lock-jawed one and assessed the situation immediately.

"Everything okay in here?" Nadia asked.

"No, not really," Sydney said, never taking her accusatory eyes off Marshall. "We need those files in half that time, maybe less. Didn't you hear Sloane's description of the virus? This is Weiss we're talking about."

"Syd, I know," Marshall said. "I'm doing everything I can—"

"Well, obviously it's not enough!" Sydney exclaimed.

"Sydney, maybe we should leave Marshall alone," Nadia suggested in a soothing tone. "I think you may need to take a break."

"Take a break? Who are you to tell me when I need to take a break?" Sydney blurted, whirling on her sister.

Nadia simply raised her eyebrows at Sydney. "Listen to yourself," she said calmly.

Sydney bit back another wave of ire. If there was one thing she couldn't stand, it was when someone talked down to her. But she forced herself to take a deep breath and regroup. Much to her chagrin, she realized that Nadia was right. She was letting her emotions rule her actions. Marshall was the best in the business, and he cared about Weiss as much as the rest of them did. She knew he was doing his best to get to Bergin's files. There was no reason to take her frustration out on him.

Feeling like a complete jerk, Sydney turned to Marshall again. "I'm sorry I snapped at you," she said. "Please come get me as soon as you have anything."

Marshall gave her a small smile. He understood. "I will," he told her.

With a parting glance at Nadia, Sydney turned and walked out of the room. At the moment, Sydney couldn't bear to be around her sister. It wasn't just that Nadia had scolded her—that was bad enough. Sydney had a hard time taking criticism from her superiors, let alone from a new agent—even if that new agent was her flesh and blood. Something else was bugging Sydney as well. Nadia's cool demeanor. How could she be so calm? Weiss was her friend, too. Wasn't she worried at all?

Sydney went to her desk and sat down, breathing deeply until she felt her pulse start to slow to a normal rate. She watched as Nadia emerged from Marshall's office, went to her desk, and started to type at her computer, cool as the other side of the pillow.

Sydney looked at her own computer screen. She still had to file her report on the Bergin debacle, but the very idea of sitting still and trying to concentrate made her ill. If only she could find that calm space that Nadia was functioning in. If only she could put everything else aside. She realized with a start that she was actually envious of her sister's ability to rise above the horror of Weiss's condition.

She's good, Sydney thought, glancing at Nadia again, whose forehead was creased with concentration. *She's really good.*

"I can't believe that even with the entire office working on this we've come up with nothing," Sydney said, leaning her head against her hand. She was exhausted. The emotional upheaval of the last couple of hours had taken a lot out of her. Something was going to have to give her a second wind or she was going to cross the line from ineffective to utterly useless.

"Bergin has had practically zero contact with the outside world. He spent every waking hour of his life in that lab," Vaughn said. He tossed the papers he was flipping through onto the desk in front of him.

"No wonder he was such a social disaster at his party," Sydney said.

"Seriously. According to his credit card records, the only people he sees are the delivery guys from Jimmy's Burritos and Pizza Master. So unless he's dealing the VX411 to a seventeen-year-old high school dropout . . ."

"Speaking of pizza, should Weiss really be eating all this junk food?" Sydney asked.

Vaughn followed her gaze to the small monitor on the table in front of them. The feed came from the discreet surveillance camera mounted in the corner of Weiss's room. Nadia was down there with him right now, and they were both laughing over a huge pizza pie loaded down with every topping imaginable.

"The doctors said he could have whatever he wants," Vaughn said. "I think Weiss is viewing every meal as potentially being his last."

Sydney took a sharp breath. "God, I wish there was something we could do for him."

The sound on the monitor was turned all the way down, but even without dialogue, Sydney could tell that Nadia was doing an excellent job of cheering up the patient.

"At least she's got him laughing," Vaughn said.

"Yep. All I did when I went down there was depress the heck out of him," Sydney said, picking up a pencil and tapping it on the desk.

"I'm sure that's not true," Vaughn said, leaning toward her.

"You weren't there," Sydney replied. "They may as well have been playing the funeral dirge when I left."

Vaughn reached out and gently tucked a lock of hair behind Sydney's ear, letting his thumb linger along her cheek. Sydney took a deep breath and savored the contact. It was amazing how a little touch from Vaughn could be so infinitely comforting.

"I got it!" Marshall shouted from the back of the office.

Sydney raised her head at the commotion, and she and Vaughn were on their feet as Marshall rushed over to them, waving a piece of paper over his head.

"I got it!" he repeated triumphantly. His grin was a mile wide. "I have the names of Bergin's financers."

Sydney's heart took an excited leap as she and Vaughn exchanged a look. This was the break they had been hoping for. A real lead.

"Come on. Sloane's waiting for us," Marshall said, practically skipping as he led the way to the conference room.

Sydney glanced at the monitor as she followed Marshall and Vaughn. Nadia and Weiss were still deep in conversation, and she decided not to disturb them. Keeping Weiss in good spirits was as important a task as any.

Dixon was already standing in the center of the room when Sydney and the others walked in. Jack slipped in right behind them and hovered next to Sydney. It seemed as if everyone was too anxious to sit. Sloane hung up his cell phone and turned to face them.

"Marshall? What do you have for us?" Sloane asked.

"Okay, it looks like Bergin had two major backers," Marshall said, clearly savoring this opportunity to announce his breakthrough. "The first is a man named Ian McMurtray. He's deposited more than two million dollars in Bergin's accounts over the past year or so, but I don't think he's our guy."

"And why not?" Sloane asked.

"Because the second backer—get this—has paid Bergin *fifty million dollars* over the past *two* years," Marshall said. "I don't know about you guys, but that sounds like terrorist money to me."

"Who is he?" Sydney asked.

"His name is Peter Land," Marshall said. "He's some South African mega-mogul."

Sloane's face went slack, and Sydney recognized the name instantly.

"No," Sloane said. "Peter Land is not our man."

Marshall's brow creased, and he glanced down at his findings. "I really think he is, Mr. Sloane. The sheer amount of his transfers and the—"

"Marshall, Peter Land is a good man and a world-renowned philanthropist," Sloane said tersely. "I worked with him closely when I was at Omnifam. His company is a leading supplier of bulk food supplies to sports venues, schools, and hospitals all over Africa, and he has donated billions of dollars' worth of food to the AIDS-ravaged villages on that continent. He is not a terrorist."

Marshall looked completely deflated. He sat down hard on the couch behind him, staring at his paper. "Well, the only other significant money came from this Ian McMurtray guy."

"Did you run his name?" Vaughn asked.

"I'm *still* running it," Marshall replied with a

shrug. "So far we've just got a list of random dudes around the globe with that same name. No one suspect, and no one who could afford a two-million-dollar donation to science."

"So we're back to Peter Land," Dixon said.

"You know, Arvin, this wouldn't be the first time that we encountered a person who is not quite the angel he seems to be," Sydney's father said pointedly.

Sydney savored the moment as Jack's comment hit home, watching Sloane as he tried not to react. As one of the most evil and prolific terrorists of his time, Sloane had kept up a perfect front for years masquerading as a top CIA operative. So many people had believed he was a true patriot—including Sydney—when, in fact, he had been a sworn enemy of the United States working within its borders. It was thanks to Sloane that Sydney had learned firsthand that she couldn't always trust her instincts.

This time, however, she couldn't help but agree with Sloane—no matter how much it irritated her.

"I don't know," she said, stepping away from the wall. "I met Peter Land last year. He helped the CIA gain access to a prison in South Africa so we could free one of our agents. He's such a kind, peaceful, thoughtful man. I can't imagine he would finance something as insidious as VX411."

"Well, what else could he have been paying for?" Dixon asked.

"Any number of things," Sloane interjected. "That's what we need to find out." He sat forward and laced his fingers together on the table. "Sydney, as you pointed out, you've met with Land before. I'd like you to go see him and find out what, exactly, his ties are to Dr. Bergin. Perhaps you can enlist his help in finding Dr. Bergin. He may even know who this elusive Mr. McMurtray is."

"Arvin, I hate to contradict you, of course, but do you really think that sending Sydney to South Africa is the best use of our resources?" Jack asked. "We are on a short time line here."

"I want to go," Sydney said firmly. She finally felt like there was something she could do—some active and productive way in which she could help Weiss. "Land is very old-fashioned. He appreciates face-to-face meetings. If I go there in person I'll have a much better chance of securing his assistance."

"I agree," Sloane said, standing. "Sydney, we'll have a plane ready for you in one hour."

CHAPTER 5

Sydney walked quickly through the airy lobby of the Hillbrow building in Johannesburg, where Peter Land's office was. The flight had been long and bumpy, affording little time for rest but plenty of time for thought. Sydney had read over Peter Land's file, and while there was nothing to suggest that he may have terrorist ties, she had resolved to treat him like any other suspect. She couldn't go into this meeting thinking she was going to see a friend. If she went in with that kind of bias, she might miss something important—

something that could be critical to Eric Weiss's survival.

He may have a long list of good works under his belt, but that could all be a smoke screen, Sydney told herself as she entered the sleek silver elevator and hit the button for the top floor. If there was one thing she had learned in her years as an agent, it was that things were often not as they seemed.

The elevator doors slid open, and Peter Land stood waiting for her at the front desk with a grandfatherly smile. Broad and potbellied with salt-and-pepper hair and a bushy mustache, Peter Land cut a very unsinister figure.

"Sydney Bristow!" he said, extending his hand. "So good to see you again."

"Mr. Land," Sydney said. His handshake was warm and firm.

"What brings you to our fair city?" he asked, ushering her toward his office. "It's an exciting time to visit, with all the exhibition matches being played. Are you a fan of football, Ms. Bristow?"

"American football, yes," Sydney said with a small smile. "Soccer, unfortunately, puts me to sleep."

"Oh, it pains me to hear you say that," Mr. Land said as he opened a frosted-glass door for her, holding one hand over his heart. "In fact, you should probably not say those words outside this office. Our people are very passionate about the national squad."

Sydney stepped into his modern office and waited for him to take a seat behind his desk. Instead, Mr. Land walked over to a plush leather couch in the corner and sat back, unfastening the button on his suit jacket. He looked as comfortable as a man chatting with an old friend in his living room. If he suspected that she was here to talk to him about Bergin, he wasn't giving any outward signs of discomfort or nervousness.

"Soccer, as you call it, is a game of endurance," Land said, resting his arm on the back of the couch. "I would think that a woman in your profession would appreciate that."

"Excuse me for being so abrupt, Mr. Land, but unfortunately I don't have time to debate sports right now," Sydney said standing on the opposite side of his glass-topped coffee table. "I've come here to talk to you about Dr. Lance Bergin."

"Ah, Dr. Bergin," Land said with a small smile and a nod. "I suspected as much. Please, Ms. Bristow, have a seat. We will talk about my dealings with Dr. Bergin."

"Thank you, I think I'll stand," Sydney said, not wanting to give up the natural advantage that height offered.

"Whatever you prefer," Land replied, maintaining his casual pose. "What is it you wish to know?"

"We have intel that you have paid Bergin huge sums of money over the past two years. Fifty million American dollars, to be exact," Sydney said, watching closely for Land's reaction. He didn't blink. "What, exactly, was he working on for you?"

Peter Land took a deep breath. He placed both feet on the floor and sat forward, resting his forearms on his knees.

"Lance Bergin was working on a revolutionary AIDS vaccine," he said, adjusting his tie so that it fell straight. "He had some radical ideas. Ideas neither your government nor mine were willing to hear. I subsidized his work."

"An AIDS vaccine," Sydney said. He was fidgeting, but not in a suspicious or over-the-top way.

"Ms. Bristow, you know that I donate millions of dollars' worth of food and clothing to AIDS victims all over Africa each year," Land said, sitting up straight and folding his hands on his lap. "I visit these villages. I see the faces of these women who have only days to live, who know they are leaving their children alone to suffer. I do everything I can to help them, but it's not enough. Someone has to find the cure. I believe that Lance Bergin was close to a breakthrough."

"Was?" Sydney prompted.

Land smiled slightly as he looked up at her. "You and I both know that Dr. Bergin has recently gone missing. I receive the newswires from the States."

His amusement was getting under Sydney's skin.

"Mr. Land," Sydney said, staring him directly in the eye. "Do you have any idea where Dr. Bergin is at this time?"

"I'm sorry, Ms. Bristow, I don't," Land replied. "Believe me when I tell you I'm very interested in finding him myself. I have, after all, invested a lot of money in him."

Yes. Maybe too much money for a philanthropic endeavor, Sydney thought. Unfortunately, Land was giving her nothing to latch on to. It was time to put all her cards on the table.

"Dr. Bergin has constructed a very deadly bioweapon. Do you know anything about that?" she asked.

Land's soft features creased with concern. "A bioweapon?"

"Yes. A bioweapon that another agent—a good friend of mine—has been exposed to," Sydney replied, trying not to dwell on the picture of a weakened and feverish Eric Weiss that flitted through her mind.

"I know nothing about a bioweapon," Peter Land said. "Are you sure it's Bergin's work?"

"I'm sure," Sydney said, her mind returning to images from that night in the lab: Bergin cutting a slit in Eric's protective gear, the vial breaking.

"I can't believe that Dr. Bergin would waste his time with such things," Land said, standing and crossing to the window. "Why would a man capable of doing such good want to create such an atrocity?" he asked, looking at her over his shoulder.

That's what I'd like to know, Sydney thought. "Mr. Land, if you have any idea where Bergin might be, I need to know. My friend's life depends on it."

Land turned his back to the window and faced her, his eyes kind. "I'm so sorry, Ms. Bristow, but I can't help you. Dr. Bergin and I are not friends. I know nothing about him above and beyond his brilliance."

Sydney's heart sank. "Are you sure? Think back over your conversations. Even a small detail that might seem unimportant could help us find him."

Slowly, Peter Land shrugged, shaking his head as he racked his brain. "We spoke of nothing but his progress."

Sydney sighed, resigned. She had no choice but to believe him. He was exhibiting none of the classic outward tells of a person who was lying. The man was either innocent, or one of the best actors Sydney had ever encountered.

The very thought of leaving there empty-handed made Sydney want to crawl into a hole and hide until it was all over. So far, she had failed Weiss in every possible way.

"I'm sorry, Ms. Bristow," Land said. "I wish there was something I could do."

Sydney tried to smile, but it felt forced and strained. "Thank you for your time."

"If there's anything else I can—"

"Actually, there is one thing," Sydney said. "There was another name connected to Bergin— another donor: Ian McMurtray. Does that name mean anything to you?"

She could tell that Land recognized the name

before he even spoke. "Ian McMurtray?" he said, the color draining from his face.

"You know him," Sydney said.

"Ms. Bristow, Ian McMurtray is an alias. The man's real name is Houtan Assin," Land told her. "If Bergin was working with him, then he must be your man. He is not a person to be trifled with."

"Who is he?" Sydney asked.

"Assin is a Turkish terrorist," Land said, stepping away from the window. "I used to know him in diplomatic circles before he turned radical. The last I heard of him he was lying low in Ireland, running a pub or some such nonsense, thus the Irish alias. Ms. Bristow, if anyone is financing a bioweapon, it's Assin. I suggest you find him, and quickly."

Sydney nodded, grateful to have a new lead and a source of new hope. "Thank you, Mr. Land."

"Of course," he said, extending his hand again. When Sydney took it, he cupped their hands with his other palm. "Ms. Bristow, I do hope your friend will be all right."

"Thank you," Sydney said, touched by his kindness.

"And I hope that next time we meet, it will be

under much more joyous circumstances," he said.

Sydney smiled, gave him a small nod, and left the room. She was dialing Marshall before she even reached the elevator. She had to put him on Assin's trail right away.

"Run the name now and call me back, okay?" Sydney said into her cell phone as she crossed the lobby. "I want you guys to keep me posted on any developments. I should be on the return flight in forty-five minutes."

"You got it, Syd," Marshall said. "Good work."

We'll see, Sydney thought as she flipped her phone closed.

As she headed for the security desk to return her guest pass, a man talking with the guard on duty caught her eye. She could only see his profile, but there was no doubt in her mind she had seen this man before. Sydney's internal warning system went off. This person didn't belong here. Wherever she had seen him last, he was now completely out of context.

Sydney slowed her steps, and the man turned around as the security officer typed away at her computer. Now Sydney had a full view of the man's

face—the slackening skin of his cheeks, the reced-
ing blond hairline, the wire-rimmed glasses, his
bored expression. Suddenly it hit her with full
force: This man was at Bergin's party. He had been
standing near Vaughn at the bar talking to some
science professors and had whispered something in
Bergin's ear just as he entered the room. What was
he doing here, in Johannesburg?

*He's obviously close to Bergin. He must be
here to see Land on Bergin's behalf,* Sydney
thought, her pulse skyrocketing. *This can't be a
coincidence.*

Before she could even ponder the fact that she
had just let Peter Land dupe her, Sydney sprang
into action. She wasn't sure yet what it all meant,
but she knew that if she didn't act fast, she was
never going to find out. Sydney spotted a small
area of wet floor that was marked off by a yellow
cone. The janitor was working his way toward the
wall with his mop, his back to the lobby. Sydney
opened her purse and riffled through it as she
walked, pretending to be searching for her keys.
Out of the corner of her eye she saw the man step
away from the security desk with his clearance
pass. She had to time this perfectly.

Just as the man was about to pass by her, Sydney stepped on a patch of wet floor and went down. She let out a startled cry as the contents of her purse scattered everywhere. Now all she had to do was hope that this friend of Bergin's was a gentleman.

"Miss! Are you all right?"

Gotcha, Sydney thought.

As the man reached down to grasp Sydney's arm, she quickly reached into her pocket and pulled out a tiny circular pad that Marshall had given her before she left L.A. It was an invisible microphone that could be placed on any piece of clothing and would remain functional until the garment was washed. As Sydney struggled to her feet, grasping the man's shoulders and laughing in embarrassment, she peeled the tiny bug from its backing and planted it right under the lapel of his jacket.

"Thank you so much," she gushed as he helped her to one of the benches that surrounded a small fountain at the center of the lobby. "I should really watch my step."

"It's no problem," the man said, quickly gathering her things. He handed Sydney her purse and smiled in a perfunctory way. "It was my pleasure."

Sydney smiled brightly as the man walked briskly toward the elevators. "The pleasure's all mine," she said under her breath.

She stood up as she saw one of the security guards headed her way, an ingratiating look of concern on her face. Sydney smiled and handed the woman her security pass. "I'm fine. Thank you," she said. On her way out the door she flipped open her phone and hit her speed-dial button for Marshall.

"Syd! What's up? I'm still running the name. I mean, I'm good, but not that good."

"I'm not calling about Assin. Activate that mic you gave me," Sydney said as she emerged from the building and into the sunshine. "Land may still be our man."

Sydney took a seat on a marble bench in the open courtyard across the street from Land's building. She pulled a paperback book out of her bag, crossed her legs at the ankles, and pretended to read. Any passerby would have thought she was a businesswoman on her lunch break, enjoying a few moments' peace. In fact, Marshall was chatting away in her ear as he linked the invisible micro-phone up to a speaker back at APO so that Vaughn, Nadia, and Jack could listen in to Land's conversa-tion with Bergin's associate.

"Okay, we are up and running," Marshall said.

Sydney slowly turned the page of her book. Her heart pounded in her chest. *Land tricked me,* she thought over and over again. *How could I have been so wrong about him?*

"Sydney, you say you saw this man at Lance Bergin's party," her father said in her ear. "Any idea who he is?"

"None," Sydney said, barely moving her lips. "But he was basically the only person besides me who got close to Bergin. They must know each other well."

Over the microphone, Sydney and the others heard the man greet the receptionist at Land's office.

"Well, it looks like we're about to find out," Nadia said.

"Mr. Land, I am Ryan Markenson."

"Running the name," Marshall said.

"A pleasure to meet you," Peter Land's voice crackled over Sydney's earpiece.

Sydney held her breath and listened. Part of her hoped that her instincts had been right about Land—that he was, in fact, a good man. But another part of her hoped that she had been wrong. If Land was their bad guy, she would be that much closer to finding information that might help Weiss.

"*I trust you have good news for me, Mr. Markenson,*" Land said.

"*Dr. Bergin has sent me to assure you that everything is right on schedule,*" Markenson said. "*Contrary to what you may have heard, Dr. Bergin will be here, as planned, for your meeting tomorrow night.*"

"*I am relieved to hear it,*" Land said. "*And will he have the samples with him?*"

Sydney's heart slammed against her rib cage. The samples. Bergin was going to deliver samples to Land. But samples of what? Was it the VX411, or was it samples of the AIDS vaccine Land had told her about?

"*Yes. The transaction will go forward as planned,*" Markenson said.

"*Good. I trust I will be pleased?*" Land asked.

"*Very,*" Markenson said. "*It is a . . . unique product.*"

"*I'm sure it is,*" Land replied. "*Well, please*

give Dr. Bergin my best. I am happy to hear that he is safe, and I will see him tomorrow night."

"I will, sir. Thank you."

Sydney heard the sound of a door closing and she finally started to breathe again.

"Well, that's it," Vaughn said. "Land is clearly our guy."

"We still don't know that for sure," Sydney replied. "They could have been talking about samples of the AIDS vaccine Land said he was paying Bergin to create."

"It's possible, but not probable," Nadia said. "Sydney, if Land knew he had a meeting scheduled with Bergin for tomorrow night, why didn't he tell you? He would have no reason to hide that unless he was dealing in something illegal."

Sydney swallowed hard. Nadia had a good point.

"Okay . . . well, at least we know that he's meeting Bergin tomorrow night," Sydney said. "All we have to do is keep an eye on Land and he'll lead us straight to Bergin and the vaccine."

"If we have that long," Sydney's father said matter-of-factly.

Sydney's stomach dropped at his words. Who

knew how long they had before Weiss took a turn for the worse? Thanks to Bergin's disappearing act, APO was flying blind.

Across the street, the door to Land's office building opened and Markenson stepped out, trading his spectacles for a pair of dark sunglasses. Sydney was on her feet instantly, an idea forming in her mind. She shoved her things into her bag and headed for the edge of the courtyard.

"I have Markenson in my sights," she said. "I'm going to follow him."

"Sydney, I'm not sure that's a good idea," her father said.

"If Bergin is meeting Land in Johannesburg, it's possible that he's already here," Sydney said, jogging across the street just as the light turned red. "Markenson might lead me right to him."

"All right, Sydney, but be careful," her father said. "You cannot be seen."

"I know, Dad," Sydney said. *I have done this before.*

"Sydney, you're our only agent in Johannesburg," her father said. "If Markenson sees you, he'll know you're onto him. They might call the whole thing off."

"Got it," Sydney said. "I'll be careful."

Her mark turned down the side street, where Sydney's black Audi was parked. *Very helpful of him,* Sydney thought. She jogged to the corner and saw him enter a parking garage. She jumped into her car and pulled it up to the curb on the opposite side of the street, where she had a perfect view of the garage's exit. Sitting low in her seat, she watched and waited.

A few moments later, a red BMW paused at the end of the exit ramp and waited for a truck to pass by. Sydney sat up straight and put the car in drive. It was Markenson.

At least he picked a car that's going to be hard to lose, Sydney thought as she pulled out behind him. At the end of the block, Markenson made a right and stopped at a light. Sydney flipped down the visor to shield her face. Markenson had gotten a good look at her when he had helped her up off the floor. If he happened to glance in his rearview mirror and saw her right behind him in traffic, he might get suspicious.

The light turned green, and Markenson took off. The side streets in this area of Johannesburg were tight and lined with cars. Pedestrians jammed the sidewalks and crosswalks. Vendors sold fresh fruit on street corners, and teenagers hung out in packs, kicking soccer balls back and forth or listening to music. For the first few blocks, the chase was anything but high speed. Sydney found herself hoping that Markenson would turn onto the highway that snaked around the city, just so that she might camouflage herself behind another car for a mile or so. Markenson was making a lot of turns, and a keen man would soon notice that the car behind him had been there for one too many detours.

Finally Markenson made a left onto a wider, two-lane road, banked by apartment buildings and trees. He picked up speed, and Sydney dropped back a bit, trying to remain inconspicuous. At the next stoplight, she saw Markenson open a city map onto his dashboard.

"Does this guy even know where he's going?" Sydney said under her breath. She hit a couple buttons on her own high-tech GPS system and brought up a search for area hotels, checking to see if there was any obvious clue as to where Bergin might be staying. There were no hotels or motels within a twenty-mile radius. She was sitting smack in the middle of a residential district.

REPLACED

Come on, Markenson. Where's your boss?
Sydney thought.

The light turned green, and Markenson didn't move. He was still poring over his map. Sydney glanced in the rearview mirror. There was a delivery truck right behind her with a line of cars forming at its rear. The delivery truck edged toward her bumper, the driver's face creased with impatience.

"Don't honk," Sydney urged quietly. "Please don't—"

The truck driver leaned on his horn, and Sydney ducked down just as she saw Markenson's eyes in his rearview mirror.

He didn't see me. He couldn't have seen me, Sydney thought as the truck engine behind her revved. When she sat up again, Markenson had passed through the intersection and the truck driver was again leaning on his horn, this time for her.

Sydney hit the gas and sped after Markenson. He wasn't driving erratically, so she was still in the clear. Up ahead, throngs of children in starched uniforms poured out of a school and flooded the sidewalk. Markenson was pausing at another red light. Suddenly, a pair of little girls shot out into the street right in front of Sydney's car. She slammed on her brakes, her heart in her throat. Both girls froze in terror as the car skidded to a stop, tires screeching.

Sydney looked at the girls. Their eyes were wide as saucers, but they were fine. Gripping the steering wheel, Sydney turned her attention to the red BMW, hoping Markenson had been too distracted to notice her near accident. No such luck. Markenson was looking right at her in the rearview mirror. And from the expression on his face, he knew exactly why she was there.

Sydney had no choice now. She had to take this guy into custody and interrogate him so that she could find out where Bergin was. There was no other option. She could not, under any circumstances, lose sight of Markenson.

The schoolgirls tottered to the other side of the street, their knees visibly shaking. The light turned green. Markenson jammed his car into gear, and the chase was on.

Markenson made a right and then a quick left, his rear tires skidding as he splashed through a puddle left by a running hose. Flying up to a T intersection, he blasted right over the crosswalk, narrowly missing a young couple who had to dive out of the way. They were still on the ground when Sydney careened by them and jammed her steering wheel to the right. Up ahead, Markenson zoomed into a traffic circle and popped his right wheels up onto the sidewalk, accelerating past the slower moving vehicles that were inching their way to their exits.

This guy is not messing around, Sydney thought, following his lead and nearly taking off her side mirror on a lamppost. Markenson took a sharp right and exited onto a two-lane one-way street—going in the wrong direction.

Cars swerved left and right, trying to get out of the way as Markenson barreled right up the center of the street, parting traffic. Sydney raced after him and dodged the fishtailing cars, ignoring the angry drivers. Up ahead, Markenson slammed on his brakes and made a hard right, zooming the wrong way up an exit ramp from the eight-lane highway ahead. A pickup truck slammed on its brakes, and the car behind it smashed into its rear bumper. Sydney barely made it past the accident and made another hard right to join the traffic on the highway. Markenson dodged and weaved in and out of traffic, putting more and more distance between himself and Sydney.

At least we're going in the right direction now, Sydney thought, mirroring his every move. Traveling in the left lane now, Sydney pushed the engine to its limit, accelerating until she was right on Markenson's tail. He glanced in the rearview, took one look at her, and suddenly veered right. Sydney's eyes widened. The van in the next lane of traffic slammed on its brakes, turned sideways, and flipped over. The cars in the next two lanes hit the brakes as well, and car after car slammed into one another as Sydney chased Markenson across all four lanes of traffic. Clipping the rear of his car on a guardrail, Markenson barely made it onto an exit ramp and raced back down into the city.

Sydney gripped the wheel tightly as she glanced in her mirror and saw the destruction that she and Markenson had just left in their wake. This guy did not want to get caught, but now, more than ever, she was determined to not let him get away.

Back on the city streets, Markenson ran a red light and took a left, once again heading the wrong way down a one-way street. This one was narrow, with cars parked along either side. It was all Sydney could do to keep from whooping in triumph. Markenson had just made a fatal mistake.

Up ahead, a car headed right for the BMW. There was nowhere for Markenson to go. He was going to have to stop his car and get out. *It looks like I might be in for a footrace,* Sydney thought. Judging by his size and age, she had a feeling she would have a distinct advantage. This guy was done.

The car ahead kept coming toward them. If one of the drivers didn't stop soon, there was going to be a head-on collision. What did Markenson think he was doing? And then, Sydney saw it. Up ahead on the left was a narrow entrance to what appeared to be a garbage-littered alleyway. Markenson looked at her in the rearview mirror.

You must be kidding, she thought.

Markenson slammed on his brakes and took the turn, slamming the side of the BMW into the far wall of the alley. Sparks flew as the driver's side door scraped against the bricks, but he made it. He accelerated down the alley to who knew where.

"Dammit!" Sydney said under her breath. She downshifted, turned the wheel, and just missed the oncoming car.

Markenson had a good lead on her now. Sydney gunned the engine. At the end of the alley, traffic zoomed by. Markenson careened onto the road without pause, just inches in front of a white van. The startled driver slammed on his brakes, and blocked the end of the alley.

"Oh, no," Sydney shouted. "No!"

She hit her brakes and jammed the heel of her hand against the horn. "Get out of the way!" she yelled, honking over and over again. "Get out! Go!"

The driver looked at Sydney, confused. Finally she threw up her hands and inched the van up and to the side of the road. Sydney lurched forward and finally emerged onto the street. She made a right, following in the same direction Markenson had taken, but the red BMW was nowhere in sight.

"Come on . . . come on," Sydney said, her pulse racing.

She could not have just lost her only connection to Bergin. Sydney came to the end of the street and frantically looked both ways. The road snaked off to the left and the right. Cars whooshed by in both directions at top speed. Whichever way Markenson had gone, he had long since disappeared.

Sydney slammed the heel of her hand against the steering wheel. Her next conversation with APO was not going to be pretty.

CHAPTER 6

Sydney sat back in the hard, uncomfortable desk chair in her hotel suite and watched as Arvin Sloane reacted to her report from thousands of miles away. The heavy damask curtains had been pulled over the plateglass window behind her to block the sunlight so that she could clearly see the screen, and it made the hotel room feel dark and gloomy. Although Vaughn, Dixon, Nadia, and her father were all sitting in on the video conference call, Sloane's face was the only one on Sydney's laptop screen. Predictably, he did not look pleased.

"Sydney, this is not good news," he said, lifting his chin.

"I did everything I could," Sydney replied, struggling to keep her anger at herself and her humiliation over another job poorly done under control. She had had Markenson in her grasp and had let him slip away. There was no one to blame but herself.

"We know you did, Sydney," her father said.

Sydney took a calming breath. "How's Weiss doing?"

After a short pause, Vaughn answered. "His condition is worsening," he said. "They're trying to keep his fever down, but he's been slipping in and out of consciousness for the last hour or so."

Sydney's heart contracted, but she kept her expression impassive, knowing they could all see her. "What's our next move?"

"Clearly we have to put someone on Land," Sloane said. "Infiltrating his meeting with Bergin tomorrow night is now our prime objective."

"I agree," Sydney said. She was about to offer her services, but Sloane cut her off.

"Sydney, since Land knows you so well and knows you are an agent, and since this Markenson now knows you were following him, I've decided to take you out of the field," Sloane said.

Sydney sat forward in her chair. "But I'm the only one here."

"You should have thought of that before you rushed off so hastily after our only lead," Sloane said.

Sydney fought to keep from grabbing the computer screen and shaking it. "What else was I supposed to—"

"Sydney, not only are both Land and Bergin now well aware that they are being watched, but they also know exactly which agent to look for," Sloane interrupted coolly. "You have compromised yourself, Sydney. I'm sending Vaughn and Nadia to South Africa to take over. You will stay in town and run their op from your hotel room."

"With all due respect," Sydney spat. "I'm perfectly capable of continuing this operation myself."

"This is my final word, Sydney," Sloane said firmly. "Vaughn and Nadia will be on a plane within the hour." He looked directly into the computer's camera lens. "I suggest you make yourself comfortable."

With that, the camera clicked off and Sydney

was left staring at the APO insignia on her desktop. She felt as if the wind had been knocked out of her. Yes, she had messed up. She knew that. But to be denied the chance to fix the situation? It was more than she could take.

Sydney stood up, slammed the laptop closed, and paced across the room. If she was taken out of the action, she was going to go crazy. She couldn't just sit in this room while Vaughn and Nadia were out executing the mission she had botched so badly. Not while Weiss grew sicker and sicker, all because of her.

"Bastard," she said under her breath, picturing Sloane's superior expression.

She sat down on the edge of the king-size bed, her heart pounding, trying not to feel so caged in and humiliated and reprimanded. She leaned forward and rested her forearms on her thighs.

Breathe in . . . count to ten . . . breathe out . . .

Sydney tried every relaxation technique in the book, but she couldn't shake her agitation. Sloane had pulled her off the mission in front of everyone. He'd basically given her a slap on the hand while the whole team sat and watched. What right did he have to second-guess her? He wasn't here. He didn't know what had happened. She was an elite field agent. Sloane knew it. Everyone knew it. Otherwise she never would have been selected to work for APO. Where did Sloane get off?

You're just displacing your anger, a little voice in her head told her. *You're mad at yourself for losing Markenson. You know Sloane was right to bench you on this one.*

Suddenly the striped wallpaper and the thick carpeting and the oversize cherry wood furniture seemed to be closing in on her. This place was too stifling. The very thought of running an op out of this room made her skin crawl.

Sydney pushed herself off the bed, adrenaline coursing through her veins. She grabbed her key card and walked out, heading for the hotel gym. It was well past time to work out a bit of her pent-up energy. She hoped this place was equipped with a few punching bags.

Marcus Dixon scanned his computer screen as account lists from various banks and mortgage holdings companies scrolled in front of him. His search through the larger companies in Johannesburg had been unenlightening so far.

Aside from the obvious—accounts for the Land Foods Corporation, and personal investment accounts belonging to Peter Land himself—there was nothing. No out-of-the-ordinary dealings, no shady transactions. So far, the guy was as clean as both Sloane and Sydney had believed he would be. If he hadn't kept his upcoming meeting with Bergin a secret from Sydney earlier that day, Dixon would have had no reason to suspect Land.

The computer beeped, and a flashing red line appeared in the center of the screen. Dixon sat up straight and pulled his chair a bit closer to his desk.

"What's this? The Moxie Corporation?" Dixon said under his breath.

He clicked on the listing, and a new Web page opened up. As he read the information displayed on the screen, his eyes slowly widened. He read through a second time, just to be sure his sleep-deprived brain wasn't making this up. Then he grabbed the phone and dialed an old contact in Johannesburg—a man who had inside knowledge of the city's red-light district and all its players. If anyone could confirm the information that Dixon had just stumbled upon, it would be Kwame Baker.

* * *

"Mr. Dixon! Mr. Dixon! You are never going to believe what I just dug up about Peter Land," Marshall called out breathlessly, running up to Marcus's desk.

"Thanks, Kwame," Dixon said into the phone and then hung up the receiver.

Dixon leaned back in his chair, raising one eyebrow. "Is it that he's a silent partner in one of the biggest strip clubs in Johannesburg?"

Marshall's face creased in confusion. "No. Is he really? Wow. This guy gets around. Check this out."

Dixon took the folder Marshall offered him and scanned its contents. Peter Land was looking more and more like a criminal every second. Dixon slapped the folder closed and stood. "We need to go to Sloane with this. Now."

They found Sloane in his well-lit office, staring off into space from behind his desk. Dixon often wondered what his director was thinking about when he found him like this, but then would remind himself that he most likely didn't want to know. It was difficult for Marcus to even reconcile the fact that he was working for Arvin Sloane, after everything the man had done. A look inside the

113

evil mastermind's brain was the last thing he needed.

"Mr. Sloane, we have some new information on Land," Dixon said, approaching the glass-topped desk.

"Yes, what is it?" Sloane asked. He placed his palms on the desk and sat forward, giving his agents his full attention.

"Well, it turns out that Peter Land is not even his real name," Marshall said excitedly. "His name is actually Petyr Olander. Petyr—with a *y*—Olander. And while Peter Land may seem like a squeaky clean philanthropist, Petyr Olander is definitely not."

Sloane cleared his throat. "Go on."

Marshall grabbed the folder out of Dixon's hands and opened it, running his finger down the first page. "Okay, forty years ago, Petyr Olander was this young, overprivileged kid living in the Netherlands in his parents' castle on a hill. He fell in with some wealthy radicals. You know the type—disgruntled prep school kids who decided to overthrow the government. Usually a bunch of hot air, right? Except this time, the kids actually put together a plot to assassinate the prime minister."

Both Dixon and Marshall looked at Sloane and waited for him to have some kind of reaction. He simply stared back at them.

"Well, anyway, he and his friends were arrested, but there wasn't enough evidence to convict them, so instead, the prime minister had them excommunicated," Marshall said. "Olander hasn't been back to his native land since, and we're talking about one of the oldest, proudest families in the Netherlands. They practically built the place. Apparently Olander has filed several appeals over the years, asking to be allowed back onto Dutch soil, but he's been turned down each time."

Once again, Marshall paused. Sloane still didn't move. Marshall looked at Dixon, baffled. Sloane wasn't excitable by nature, but one would think that this kind of news about a supposed friend and humanitarian would elicit at least a syllable.

"Mr. Sloane?" Dixon prompted. "Did you hear what Marshall said? Peter Land was involved with an assassination plot forty years ago."

"I know, Marcus," Sloane said, gazing steadily up at him.

Dixon bristled. He detested when Sloane called him by his first name. It was patronizing when anyone in a position of authority talked down to him. But when the man who had murdered his wife did it, it was a hell of a lot worse.

"Pardon me for saying so, but you don't seem surprised," Dixon said.

"That's because I'm not," Sloane replied, looking down at the desk quickly. "You see, everything Marshall just told me, I already knew."

Dixon felt as if the floor had just dropped out from underneath him. "Excuse me?"

"I knew about Peter Land's past," Sloane said matter-of-factly. "About the prime minister and the excommunication."

"And you didn't feel the need to tell us about it?" Dixon asked, taking a step forward, his fists clenching. "In that first meeting you sat there and espoused his virtues all the while knowing he was a terrorist?"

"*Was* being the operative word here, Mr. Dixon," Sloane said calmly. "Peter Land put all that behind him years and years ago. He is a changed man—no longer the misguided radical he once was."

"What gives you the right to make that judgment?" Dixon demanded. "You sent Sydney over there to chat with the man, when we should have been treating him as hostile from the beginning."

"I have seen Peter Land do more good in the past five years than most people do in a lifetime," Sloane said, glaring up at Dixon. "I do not believe that he should be judged by some ridiculous scheme he was roped into as a boy. People can change, Marcus. You should start trying to accept that."

Dixon swallowed hard, his throat hot and dry. He knew what Sloane was really saying. He knew that Sloane wanted everyone around him to think that he himself was a changed man. Unfortunately for Sloane, that was one lie Dixon was never going to believe.

"There is something else. Another little detail we've uncovered about this *changed man*," Dixon said, savoring the moment—loving the fact that he knew something Sloane did not. A little something that could wipe that superior smirk right off his boss's face.

"What's that?" Sloane asked.

"It turns out that Peter Land is a silent partner in a firm called The Moxie Corporation, based in Johannesburg," Dixon said, sliding his hands into his pockets. "Along with a well-known slumlord named Dino Moxon, Land owns and operates The Moxie Club—the biggest strip club in the entire city. From what my contact tells me, it's the place to go if you want to buy drugs, guns, women . . . among other things."

Sloane's expression darkened as Dixon related this information. Dixon did everything he could to keep from smiling in triumph.

"According to my source, Land has a VIP booth at the club every night, and tomorrow he and his partner will be holding auditions for new exotic dancers," Dixon continued. "No one gets hired without the personal approval of both Moxon and Land."

"The Moxie Club would be a perfect place for Bergin and Land to meet," Marshall put in. "Dark, loud, lots of . . . distractions," he said, raising his eyebrows.

Sloane took a deep breath and squared his shoulders. He reached for the phone and jabbed a series of buttons.

"Vaughn, Nadia, can I see you in my office, please?" Sloane said.

While most men would have averted their gaze at being so bluntly proved wrong, Sloane stared up at Dixon as they waited. Dixon stared right back.

You don't know everything, old man, Dixon thought. *You can't always win.*

It wasn't until Vaughn and Nadia stepped into the room that Sloane finally looked away.

"Thanks to some information uncovered by Marshall and Dixon, we now have a cover for you both," Sloane said, swiveling his chair to face them. He rested one elbow on his desk and brought his hand up under his chin, placing his index finger against his cheek. "Nadia, you will be auditioning for Land and his business partner, Dino Moxon, tomorrow night."

"Auditioning? For what?" Nadia asked, knitting her brows.

"A position as an exotic dancer," Sloane replied.

"What?" Vaughn said, pulling his chin back in surprise.

"Apparently, Land owns a strip club and is holding a casting call," Sloane said. "Vaughn, you will be Nadia's overprotective boyfriend. This will get you close to Land, and you'll be able to keep an eye out for Bergin. You can brief Sydney on the mission when you get to Johannesburg. Any questions?"

Nadia was shocked. The last thing any of them had expected to hear was Land's name in connection with a strip club. But she shook her head. "No, sir."

"No," Vaughn added.

"Good. You'd better get going. Your plane leaves in exactly thirty minutes," Sloane said, checking his watch. "Marshall, you'll provide Vaughn and Nadia with the information and the op tech that they need."

"Yes, sir," Marshall said, following the two agents from the room.

"Dixon, I'll need you to keep working on Land," Sloane said. "Check out every aspect of his life. Find out who he's talking to, what other characters he might have met with in the past few months. We need to come up with some worst-case scenarios. Find out where he's planning to use the VX411, and when. Clearly the Netherlands may be a target."

"Clearly," Dixon said with a touch of sarcasm. *A fact we could have been working on yesterday if you weren't such an egomaniacal control freak,* he added silently.

Sloane narrowed his eyes slightly as if he could read Dixon's mind. "You're dismissed."

* * *

Sydney dropped her half-eaten sandwich onto her plate and picked up the room service tray. She was too tense with pent-up energy to eat. She set the tray outside her door in the hallway, unable to look at it anymore. After a two-hour workout in the gym and a sprint up the twenty flights of stairs to her room, Sydney had showered and changed into comfortable black pants and a tank top. Her plan was to eat dinner, read for a little while, and then sleep until Vaughn and Nadia arrived. She should have known that she wouldn't be able to relax long enough to do any of those things. There had to be something productive she could do.

She grabbed her cell phone and was about to dial Sloane, but changed her mind. The last thing she wanted to put herself through was another lecture. Instead, she dialed Marshall.

"Hey, Syd," he said, picking up on the first ring.

"Marshall, what's going on over there?" Sydney asked, crossing her free arm over her stomach as she paced. "Any news?"

"Good and bad," Marshall said. "Vaughn and Nadia are on their way to Johannesburg, and they've got some new information on Land."

"What kind of information?" Sydney asked, intrigued.

"Oh, just that he's a former Dutch terrorist who owns a strip club in downtown Johannesburg," Marshall said. "Apparently it's a real scene. Very swank."

"You're kidding," Sydney snorted.

"I couldn't make this stuff up if I tried," Marshall replied.

"And Weiss?" Sydney asked.

"The same," Marshall said. "He came to long enough to ask for some old *Honeymooners* episodes on DVD. I just brought them down to him."

Sydney smiled sadly. "That's good, I guess."

"Well, if you believe in laughter as therapy, then Jackie Gleason's your man," Marshall said. "How's everything going with you?"

Sydney lowered herself into a chair and ran her hand over her bangs, smoothing back her ponytail. She blew out a loud sigh. "To tell you the truth, I'm getting a little stir-crazy," she said. "I just wish there was something I could do, you know? I feel like I'm wasting my time over here."

There was a long, loaded silence, and Sydney's

shoulders tensed with anticipation. She could practically hear the gears in Marshall's mind cranking away.

"Marshall, what is it?" Sydney asked.

"Nothing," Marshall said quickly.

"No, if there's something you think I could be doing, please tell me," Sydney said. "This hotel room is closing in on me. You'd be saving me from a meltdown."

"I really shouldn't, Syd. Sloane—"

"Forget Sloane," Sydney interrupted. "What do you need?"

"Well, there *is* a little something . . . ," Marshall said reluctantly. "It might help speed things up when Vaughn and Nadia get there."

"What?" Sydney asked impatiently, planting her feet on the floor. "Marshall, I need to help."

"Okay, we have some satellite pictures of The Moxie Club—that's Land's strip club," Marshall said, lowering his voice. "But there's something weird. The building takes up an entire city block, but it looks like only half the space is being used for the actual club. We have no idea what's going on in the other half of the building. It could just be undeveloped space—"

"Or it could be something else," Sydney said, her imagination kicking into high gear. "A storage facility or a lab . . ."

"Exactly," Marshall said.

"This is perfect, Marshall. I can go over there, do a little recon, and find out what Land is using it for," Sydney said.

"Okay—but, Syd?" Marshall said, sounding nervous.

"I know: You never told me anything," Sydney said, pushing herself out of her chair. "Don't worry, Marshall. I'll take all the heat on this one."

"Thanks, Syd. And be careful. Dixon's intel says that Land is there pretty much every night. If he spots you—"

"I know. I'll be careful. And, really, Marshall, thank you," Sydney said, whipping open her suitcase. "I'll call you later."

She clicked off her phone, tossed it on the bed, and eyed her clothing choices. *What to wear to Johannesburg's swankest strip club?* Sydney wondered. She grabbed a wig and got to work.

The Moxie Club was clearly the place to be in Johannesburg. From blocks away, Sydney was weaving around groups of raucous men, giggling couples, towering transvestites, and gawking teenagers, all of whom seemed to be gravitating to the same central location. Sydney strutted along in her stiletto boots, her long, dark wig hiding the parts of her face that her heavy eye makeup did not conceal. She wore a black bustier, a miniskirt with fishnet stockings, and a leather jacket as she gazed at the other pedestrians with a bored, *been-there, done-that* expression.

125

She arrived at the corner diagonally across the street from The Moxie Club where two major thoroughfares met. A line of black limousines was parked in front of the entrance, the drivers gathered in a tight circle, chatting and laughing. Sydney could hear the bass line of the club's music pumping over the traffic. The main door faced the corner, and four no-nonsense bouncers slowly checked over each and every guest, looking at IDs and studying faces. Each time the door opened, the music grew louder and Sydney caught a glimpse of colorful, flashing strobe lights.

A line of anxious partyers stretched along the right wall, trailing away from Sydney. The street was brightly lit and heavily trafficked. Every so often someone would shout out their car window as they passed the line of club goers, and everyone would laugh or shout back. As Sydney stood, leaning against a lamppost and pretending to talk on her cell phone, three police cars drove slowly by in the span of fifteen minutes.

Between the police presence and the abundance of witnesses, this was not a good street for carrying out illegal activity. Even if the cops had been paid off to turn a blind eye to things like prostitution and drug use at this particular club (which was highly likely), Land would probably not want to conduct his other, more shady deals in plain sight.

Heaving a bored sigh, Sydney put her cell phone in her purse and crossed the street. She walked along the sidewalk, keeping The Moxie Club across the road to her right. A bunch of kids approached from the opposite direction, but there were fewer people milling around on this side of the building. The bouncers were careful to keep the line of patrons on the other side of the block. As Sydney came to the next corner, she saw why. The street that ran down the back of the building, to the north, was narrow and dark—practically an alleyway. The old brick road had yet to be paved over, and every few feet a group of bricks stuck up at an angle, creating dangerous bumps. No one would be driving down that road unless they absolutely had to.

Just as Sydney made this assessment, a black sedan pulled into the tiny street and stopped. The engine was silenced. Sydney pulled out her camera phone again and zoomed in on the driver as he stepped from the car. He was a tall, broad man in thick glasses, wearing a black suit and black shirt.

The passenger side door opened and out stepped another man—angular, slim, with a goatee and slicked-back blond hair. She took a few pictures, capturing their images so she could run them through the APO database later.

The slimmer man glanced around, checking the area, and although Sydney was sure he wouldn't be suspicious of her all the way across the street, she brought the phone to her ear and looked away. The door to the bar behind Sydney opened, and a group of loud, drunk, twenty-something men and women poured out. Sydney blended in with them as they crossed the street toward The Moxie Club.

The group veered off to join the line on the other side of the building, and Sydney broke away. Lingering near the rear bumper of the sedan, she caught a glimpse of the two men down the street, talking in low tones with a third man, someone who was fully in shadow.

Could be just a drug deal, Sydney reasoned. But her instincts told her otherwise. These guys were too well dressed to be doing a deal themselves. Plus, they were traveling in a luxury car that looked like it had just been driven off the lot. This was something else entirely.

Suddenly the three men turned and stepped into the light above an innocuous-looking metal door. Sydney could see now that the third man was Land. He had his back to her, but she would recognize that bulky frame, that perfect posture, anywhere. Land pulled a card out of his pocket and ran it through a small metal slot on a panel to the left of the door. There was a low buzzing sound, and then he opened the door and let his friends pass through, following them inside. A moment later, the door slammed behind them and, aside from the dulled music and the traffic, everything was quiet.

Sydney glanced overhead at the top corner of the building to make sure there were no surveillance cameras watching her. Taking a deep breath, she slipped past the sedan and along the wall to the door. She hoped that Land's business with those men, whatever it was, would keep him busy inside for a few minutes while she checked out the lock.

Interesting, Sydney thought as she inspected the panel. There was a small screen at the top and a slot along the side for the key card. No touchpad. There were also no visible wires or switches. Sydney had never seen anything like it. She whipped out her phone and speed-dialed Marshall.

"Syd! What's up?" Marshall whispered.

"There's a strange lock at the back entrance of Land's building," Sydney replied, also in a whisper. "I just saw him use a key card to get in, but this thing is state of the art."

"Ooh, a challenge. Describe it to me," Marshall said.

"It's a metal panel with a blank green screen," Sydney told him. "Nothing else but the slot for the key card."

"Yeah, sounds like a Micron 3000 series," Marshall said. "Man, these guys spare no expense. There must be something going on inside that they really don't want anyone else to see."

"Micron 3000," Sydney said. "Should I know what that means?"

"Only if you spend twenty-four hours a day in the hacker network chat rooms like I do," Marshall replied. "Basically no one has figured out how to override this one yet. Any attempts to hack in, and the whole thing will shut down. Without a unique key card, it's impossible to penetrate."

"Impossible. That's always a good word to hear," Sydney said.

"Hey, at least we know what we need now," Marshall replied. "Either Vaughn or Nadia is gonna have to lift a card. Good work, Sydney."

"Thanks, Marshall," Sydney said with a smile. He was right. Her little recon excursion had knocked some precious fact-finding time off Vaughn and Nadia's mission. Finally, she had done something productive. So much for Sloane telling her to stay in her room. She turned and headed back toward the main road. "I'm glad I could—"

"Sydney, where, may I ask, are you?" Sloane barked in Sydney's ear.

Her heart took a nosedive, and she paused at the corner. How the hell did he get on the line?

"You are not, I understand, in your hotel room?" he asked.

Setting her jaw, Sydney braced herself. A pair of gorgeous women strutted by, glancing at her out of the corners of their eyes.

"I'm at The Moxie Club, actually," Sydney replied casually, trying to look like a girl who was just chatting with friends. "You guys should totally come down here. It's a scene."

"Sydney, I want you to get the hell out of there right now," Sloane said. "I told you to stay out of sight. I gave you a direct order. If you have been seen . . . if you have compromised this mission, millions of lives could be at stake. That includes Agent Weiss."

Sydney felt a pang of doubt in her chest and looked up again. What if there was some kind of surveillance not visible to the naked eye? What if Land was watching her right now? Whatever was going on inside the back of this building, he may be able to move the operation and disappear, just like Bergin had. She swung her hair in front of her face and ducked her head.

"Okay," Sydney said jovially, starting across the street as the light turned green. "I'm on my way!"

"And Sydney, disobey me again and you will not want to come back to this office," Sloane warned her.

Sydney was about to bark something about empty threats, but before she could, the line went dead. Frustrated and overcome with fresh guilt about Weiss, Sydney headed back to her hotel.

As much as Sydney resented Sloane's decision to send in reinforcements, she couldn't have been happier or more relieved when Vaughn and Nadia finally arrived. She opened the door of her hotel suite and laughed when she saw how Vaughn was dressed.

"What are you supposed to be, a pimp?" she asked.

He was sporting a long, red snakeskin jacket, a black shirt open at the collar, and a gold necklace. His hair was spiked up, and he wore yellow-tinted sunglasses. There was a snake tattoo painted around the side of his neck.

"Something like that," Vaughn said, enveloping her in a welcome hug. "It's good to see you," he said, holding her tightly.

"You too," Sydney said, relishing his calming presence. She inhaled the scent of his cologne and closed her eyes. Normally they would be all-business while on a mission, but Sydney knew they both needed some reassurance. At this point, she could have held him all day.

"Hello, Sydney," Nadia said, giving her sister a quick kiss on each cheek.

Nadia was wearing a floor-length fur coat, and tons of blue eye shadow with rhinestones glued at the ends of her lash line. Her hair fell in loose waves all around her shoulders, and she popped her gum as she entered the room. She looked gorgeous, in a streetwalker kind of way.

"Don't tell me . . . stripper?" Sydney asked.

"She much prefers *exotic dancer*," Vaughn said in a thick South African accent.

"He's my boyfriend," Nadia explained, shedding the coat and revealing a sexy red minidress that showed a substantial amount of cleavage.

"Ah," Sydney said, ignoring the stab of disappointment she felt at someone else calling Vaughn her boyfriend. All in a day's work. "So what's the plan?"

Vaughn dropped his briefcase on the desk and popped the latches, revealing the usual amount of surveillance gear. Sydney noticed that his nails had been painted black and then were chipped slightly. The safety was in the details.

"Land and Moxon are holding an open call for new dancers tonight," he explained. "Apparently everyone's required to perform a lap dance."

"So you're going to choose Land as your lucky man . . . ," Sydney said.

"Allowing me to get close enough to lift his key card," Nadia finished.

"Good plan," Sydney said with a nod. It sounded

like they already had everything under control. She tried to ignore the feeling of uselessness that threatened to overcome her. It was growing more and more familiar.

"Nadia, you should make sure that you flirt a little with Land when you first get there," Sydney suggested. "Act like you're attracted to him and it won't be too suspicious when you decide to dance for him."

"Yes, I had thought of that," Nadia said, applying a new coat of lipstick in the mirror. "Thanks."

"And don't try to look like an amateur while you're auditioning," Sydney told her. "They probably only get the best dancers at a place like The Moxie Club."

Nadia caught Sydney's eye in the mirror. "I know."

Sydney stared back. "Just making sure."

"Don't worry," Nadia told her firmly. "It's not like I haven't done anything like this before."

"Just trying to help," Sydney replied, her tone flat. "We can't afford any mistakes on this mission. Weiss is running out of time."

"I'm aware of all of this, Sydney," Nadia said. "We've got everything under control."

She knows what she's doing, a little voice in

Sydney's mind told her. *Stop acting like a jealous witch.*

Sydney turned away from her sister and took a deep breath, feeling foolish. She wasn't used to having her hands tied like this. She wasn't used to watching another agent take over the role that she had been playing for the past four years. For the first time in her career, she felt as if she was replaceable. Plus, the control freak inside of her was begging to take on this mission herself. What if something went wrong, something that Nadia couldn't foresee? All the missteps that had gotten them to this point were on Sydney's shoulders. She wanted to be the one to fix the situation. She wanted the chance to redeem herself.

"I'm going to keep my sunglasses on," Vaughn told her. "They've got an imbedded camera, and Marshall has linked the feed to your computer so that both you and Marshall should be able to see whatever I see."

Sydney cleared her throat and tried to focus. She crossed her arms over her chest and braced herself against a sudden chill. "You'll be keeping an eye out for Bergin?"

"Yeah," Vaughn replied. "Among other things."

Nadia pressed her earpiece into place and rearranged her long dark hair over her ears. She grabbed her coat and slid her arms into the sleeves. "We should get going," she said.

Vaughn hit a few keys on Sydney's computer. "You should be good to go," he told her. Then he gave her a quick kiss and squeezed her shoulders. "This is all going to be over soon," he said, looking into her eyes through his ridiculous glasses.

"I know," she said, trying to feel hopeful. "Good luck."

"Luck?" Vaughn said, adopting the accent again and flashing a cocky grin. He slipped his arm over Nadia's slim shoulders. "My girl doesn't need luck."

Sydney smiled wanly as Nadia waved her fingers—getting into character—and walked out. The door closed with a heavy thud, and once again, Sydney was left alone.

"I guess I'll just stay here, then," she said to the empty room. Being an agent wasn't as exciting as it used to be.

"Look, man, the auditions are closed," the behemoth bouncer told Vaughn, placing a hand flat on his chest and giving him a good, hard shove backward. The man had a shaved-bald head and the darkest skin Vaughn had ever seen. Each ear was pierced at least six times. "You and your lady are gonna have to vacate the premises."

"Not likely," Vaughn shot back, whacking the man's clublike arm aside. "We were told this was an *open* audition."

"Yeah, it was. If you'd a' gotten here two hours ago," the bouncer replied, stepping up to Vaughn in order to better illustrate his massive size advantage. "As of two hours ago, the audition is closed."

Over the wide shoulder of the bouncer, Vaughn could see inside the back room of the club. A small catwalk was set up with a pole for dancing near the very end. Women milled about, watching as one of their competitors took the stage. Vaughn could tell that the judges, Land and Moxon, must have been sitting at the end of the runway, just out of view. He had to get by Mr. Clean or this mission would be over before it had a chance to get under way. He glanced at Nadia, and hoped she got the signal.

"You touch me again, friend, and we're gonna have some trouble, you and me," Vaughn said, knocking chests with the guy.

The bouncer laughed, flashing a row of huge,

pearly white teeth, then grew instantly serious. "You no longer amuse me."

The bouncer grabbed Vaughn's left arm and twisted it behind his back, sending a dart of pain up Vaughn's arm and into his shoulder. Holding back from using his considerable hand-to-hand skills, Vaughn slammed his heavy boot down into the guy's foot. As Mr. Clean doubled over, Vaughn saw Nadia slip into the audition room. The bouncer noticed as well.

"The moment I saw you, I knew you were gonna be trouble," the bouncer said, releasing Vaughn and then grabbing him again by the upper arm. The bouncer swung Vaughn around and shoved him into the audition room. Sure enough, Peter Land was seated on a velvet bench that faced the stage, next to a younger, greasier gentleman in a pinstriped three-piece suit. Nadia had removed her coat and already had both of them enthralled.

"I'm sorry, Mr. Moxon," the bouncer said. "These two were rather persistent."

"It's no problem, Luke," Moxon said with a brief wave of his hand. Diamond rings sparkled on all four of his fingers. "You can release the gentleman. We'll let the young lady perform."

Grudgingly, Luke the bouncer let Vaughn go, giving his shoulder a little shove for good measure. Vaughn smirked at the guy and pulled down on his snakeskin jacket, cracking his neck from side to side. Victory was sweet.

Quickly, Vaughn scanned their surroundings, letting Sydney and the team back at APO see what they were dealing with. He and Nadia had passed through the main area of the club in order to get to this smaller back room where the auditions were being held. The Moxie Club was already jam-packed with people, even though it was fairly early in the evening. Bergin could very well have been there among the throng, but Vaughn hadn't seen him. The back room was far less populated, with a lot more breathing room. Fifteen women milled around near the walls or sat back on the couches, waiting their turn to audition or relaxing after they had tried out. Half a dozen men—boyfriends and pimps, most likely—were dotted about the room. There didn't appear to be any way to get in or out of the room without passing by the towering Luke.

As the girl currently strutting her stuff finished, there was a smattering of polite applause. She hopped down from the stage and hugged a wiry man with a scruffy beard, who helped her retie her halter top.

"Christov?" Nadia said, crooking her finger at Vaughn.

He squared his shoulders and approached.

"This is Mr. Moxon and Mr. Land," Nadia said, twirling her hand toward each of them. "Christov Marsh."

"How's it going?" Vaughn asked, reaching out to vigorously shake their hands, putting on a kung fu grip. "You made a wise choice seeing my Aurora. You won't be disappointed."

"I tend to agree, Mr. Marsh," Land said, sliding his eyes over Nadia's body with an appreciative smirk.

Vaughn wanted to punch him out right then and there. What an oversexed creep. Nadia, however, rewarded the man with a coy smile and a stare that said about a million things that Vaughn didn't even want to think about. He was glad, in that moment, that it was Nadia playing this part, and not Sydney. Otherwise he might not be responsible for his actions.

"Well, Aurora," Moxon said, lifting a hand toward the stage. "Please, feel free to start whenever you wish."

Nadia turned to Vaughn and handed him her fur coat. "Don't be nervous now, baby," Vaughn said, looking Nadia in the eye.

"I never am," Nadia replied with a wink.

As she turned toward the stage, Vaughn gave her a quick whack on the backside and Nadia yelped, then laughed flirtatiously before scurrying up the steps in her stilettos.

"That's my girl," Vaughn said with a grin.

"And a fine one she is," Moxon said, settling back to watch.

"Come, Mr. Marsh. Why don't you sit with us while Aurora performs?" Land suggested.

"Sure, why not?" Vaughn said. He slung Nadia's coat over the back of the couch and dropped onto the cushions. "This girl can do things with a pole that'll make your head spin," he said.

Land smiled briefly. "I can hardly wait."

The music started up and Vaughn leaned forward, the psyched and invested boyfriend. From his new vantage point, he could see inside the open flap of Land's coat. Clipped to the inside pocket was a small, silver key card.

Nadia struck a pose at the far end of the stage, and the game was on.

CHAPTER 8

"Whoa, Syd, are you watching this?" Marshall asked.

Sydney was sitting in her chair at the hotel, her back rigid, her eyes trained on her computer screen as Nadia shimmied and strutted along the catwalk at The Moxie Club. All around the stage, colorful strobe lights flashed in unison with the beat, but they weren't distracting. They only served to highlight the expert moves, the coy expression, the perfect cheekbones of the woman dancing along the runway.

"Yes, Marshall," Sydney said, her voice sounding terse.

"She's good," Marshall said. Sydney could practically hear him drooling on the other end of the line.

"Thank you for that assessment, Marshall," Sloane said over the speakerphone. "My daughter is not putting this show on for your entertainment."

"Oh, right—sorry," Marshall said quickly. "Of course not, Mr. Sloane. I was just pointing out that she's . . . you know . . . very convincing as a . . . stripper. . . ."

"Marshall, stop talking," Sydney's father said.

"Right. Good idea," Marshall said.

On the screen, Nadia grabbed the pole and executed a perfect spin, lifting both legs off the ground and landing gracefully. A man and a woman in the back corner of the room glanced at each other, clearly impressed. Sydney was starting to wonder if Nadia's earlier comment about having done this before referred to going undercover, or performing a striptease. She did look like quite the experienced professional.

"Vaughn, take another look around the room,"

Sloane instructed. "Are we sure none of these men is Bergin?"

Obligingly, Vaughn performed another sweep. There were only a few men present, and they were all either too cocky-looking or way too buff to be the sniveling scientist in disguise.

"He's not there," Sydney told them. Vaughn returned his attention to the stage.

Just as the camera trained itself on her, Nadia paused at the end of the catwalk and lifted her minidress over her head, revealing a skimpy red bra and underwear set beneath. She glanced at Vaughn, then looked off to the right, her eyes sultry, her mouth twisted into a knowing smile. As Sydney had suggested, Nadia was flirting with Land.

"Oops. Just lost Mr. Sloane," Marshall said.

"Can't say I blame him," Dixon put in. "If I had to watch my daughter do this . . ."

"Bet you're glad we got another woman on the roster, huh, Syd?" Marshall said. "That could be you right now."

Sydney took a deep breath and let it out slowly. Little did Marshall know that she would have given anything to be in Nadia's place right then. Not only was she itching to be out in the field, but she and Vaughn were a team. They had their own short-hand. They knew how to communicate with each other with barely a glance. If anything went wrong here, Nadia and Vaughn would not have that advantage.

Who're you kidding? she chided herself as Vaughn looked around the room again, performing another quick sweep. *She's a killer agent. They're going to be just fine.*

Unfortunately, that thought somehow made her feel even worse. Whether she was working with Vaughn or Dixon or Marshall or her dad, Sydney had been *the* female field agent on her team for the past few years. She was the go-to girl. The expert. The one who could take on any role, from naive English schoolgirl to German dominatrix to Pakistani arms dealer, and perform to perfection. But from the look of things, Nadia was turning out to be just as good at her job as Sydney ever was.

Sydney knew there were plenty of ace female agents out there, but she had never worked so closely with one. She had never imagined that she could be so easily replaced.

* * *

"My baby's danced all over the world, but when we heard you gentlemen were looking for new blood, I said, 'Baby, that place is for you,'" Vaughn rambled. "Isn't she gorgeous?"

"Very," Moxon said with a tight-lipped smile. Apparently Vaughn was annoying him, which was exactly what he was going for.

"I'm just not sure she has everything we need in a Moxie Club dancer," Land added, glancing away from Nadia for a millisecond.

"Whaddaya talking about?" Vaughn asked, gesturing at the catwalk. "My girl's got everything and more."

"Not to be crude, mister . . . ?"

Vaughn knew that Land remembered his name. The guy was a diplomat and businessman who understood the importance of making everyone around him feel like the most significant man in the room. By "forgetting" his name, Land was showing Vaughn exactly how *un*important he was.

"Just call me Christov," Vaughn said.

"Christov," Land repeated, looking Vaughn directly in the eye. "But we like our dancers to have a lot more real estate up top."

Vaughn hesitated a split second. Land was

talking about Nadia's breasts. He was sitting here unabashedly telling him that Nadia's breasts weren't big enough for his liking. What a complete slime. But then, what did Vaughn expect from a guy who ran a strip club and was paying millions of dollars for a biological weapon? Even worse, it seemed, Nadia was losing Land's interest. That could be a death blow to the operation.

"It's not about *size,* man," Vaughn said quickly. "My girl is all natural. No surgery, no implants. That's one hundred percent, pure, god-given beauty you've got performing for you up there."

Land frowned thoughtfully and looked at the stage again. Now was the time. Vaughn caught Nadia's eye, and she slowly came down the steps at the end of the catwalk, lifting her long hair over her shoulders and letting it tumble down her back. Vaughn wasn't entirely sure he could watch this— his friend and colleague giving a lap dance to this reprehensible old man—but he knew he had to keep his cool. This was the moment of truth.

"Show the old man what you got, baby," Vaughn said, leaning back in the couch.

Nadia sauntered over to Land and placed one foot on either side of his legs, then slowly lowered herself onto his lap. On the other side of the couch, Moxon's eyes were bright, taking in every detail. Land reached his arms around Nadia's back and placed them against her bare skin. Vaughn swallowed hard. As far as he knew, the client was forbidden to touch the dancer, but he supposed it was different for the owner of the club—the guy who could give a dancer a job or toss her out onto the street. Besides, Land's tendency to grope could work to Vaughn's advantage.

As Land shifted his position, his jacket fell open and once again, the key card was in full view. Nadia slid her hands down the front of Land's shirt. Land was riveted. Nadia's fingers were inches from the key card. They brushed the pocket, and suddenly Land seemed to snap out of his trance. He quickly reached down and buttoned his jacket closed, making it impossible for Nadia to get at the card without being completely obvious.

Damn, Vaughn thought. *Looks like we're going to plan B.*

Nadia stood up and turned around, giving Land a back view. Vaughn held his breath. Land watched Nadia dance, practically salivating. Beads of perspiration appeared along his hairline. This guy was so disgusting, Vaughn wanted to deck him.

Come on, hold back, Vaughn told himself. *Everything hinges on this.*

For a moment it looked as if Land was going to do nothing. If so, Vaughn was going to have to go to plan C. Unfortunately, he didn't have one. But then, slowly, tremblingly, Land lifted his hands.

There you go, you sleaze, Vaughn thought.

Land reached out. His palms were millimeters from Nadia's skin. That was all Vaughn needed to see.

"Hey! Back off, you son of a bitch!" he shouted, grabbing Land's arm. Nadia yelped and turned around, and Moxon jumped out of his seat and backed toward the wall. Apparently Land wouldn't be getting any help from his business partner.

"What the hell do you think you're doing?" Land shouted, staring at Vaughn's grip around his wrist. Vaughn had about five seconds before the bouncers realized what was going on.

"You can look, but you don't touch," Vaughn said. "She's a lady, you get me?"

"I strongly suggest you let go of me, young man," Land said, his face growing red. "Right now. Or there's going to be trouble."

"You want trouble?" Vaughn shouted. Then he pulled back and landed a fierce punch right across the older man's jaw.

There was a loud *crack,* and Land hit the floor hard, taking a table and drink with him. A bunch of the girls screamed and scattered while the men hung back, assessing the situation. Vaughn dove on Land and flipped him over by the lapels. His nose was awash with blood, and his eyes rolled about, confused. Vaughn reached into his jacket to grab the key card, but before he could find it, he was suddenly hauled back off Land's prone body by Luke and a new friend.

"Christov!" Nadia shouted, jumping on Luke's back just like a scrappy stripper-girlfriend might do.

As Luke whipped around, trying to free himself from Nadia's grasp, Vaughn saw a clip sticking out the back pocket of his black pants—the very same clip that held Land's key card in place inside his jacket. Vaughn had just registered this information when a huge fist slammed into his face. His vision exploded with stars, but somehow Vaughn managed to reach out and grab Luke as he went down, bringing both the bouncer and Nadia with him.

"What the—?" Luke said as he hit the floor.

In the tangle of arms and legs and Nadia's hair, Vaughn easily snatched the key card out of Luke's back pocket. He shoved it inside his own jacket and then staggered to his feet, holding his jaw.

"That's it, man. You're outta here." The tow-headed bouncer who had hit Vaughn clamped a beefy hand around his bicep.

"Fine! We don't need this gig, anyway," Vaughn said angrily as he allowed himself to be dragged toward the door. "Aurora! Let's go."

"Wait just one minute," Land called out.

Vaughn, Luke, Nadia, and the other bouncer all paused and turned to face the man in charge. He was holding a white handkerchief to his nose, and his eyes were glistening with unshed tears from the pain. Somehow, he still managed to stand up perfectly straight, and not a single white hair on his evil head was out of place.

"Aurora, you may stay," Land said, his voice made nasal by his plugged-up nose. "You have the job, if you want it. And if you keep your boyfriend here far, far away from our club. We can't have a loose cannon like him hanging around, going off like that on our clientele. But I like you. We'd love to have you on staff. What do you say?"

"Aurora" looked at her "boyfriend" uncertainly. "It *is* a lot of money. . . ."

Vaughn twisted his face into a mask of betrayal and ripped his arm away from the bouncer. "You're gonna take a job over me?"

"Christov—"

"You know, if you want to be in this business, you're going to have to learn to check your ego at the door . . . Christov," Land said, reaching out and straightening Vaughn's lapel with his free hand.

Vaughn took a deep breath and looked Land in the eye. "Fine," he said reluctantly. "I'll go. I don't want any more trouble. I'm just glad you realized my girl's talent."

Land nodded. "Make sure he makes it safely to the street," he told Luke.

"Hang on! Hang on! Can I at least talk to my girlfriend for a second?" Vaughn said, lifting his hands.

Land slid his eyes over Vaughn like he was a piece of garbage. "Make it quick."

Vaughn gave the bouncers a warning glance, then grabbed Nadia's hand and pulled her aside.

"Congratulations," he said, pulling her into a hug.

"Thanks, baby," Nadia replied.

"I have the key card," he whispered into her ear. "I'm going to check out the rest of the building. Don't let Land out of your sight. We have to nail Bergin if he shows."

Nadia nodded tearfully as if she were simply saying good-bye to Christov, then smiled as he pulled away. Out of the corner of his eye, Vaughn saw Land and Moxon watching them, so he pulled Nadia in for a long, firm kiss on the lips.

"Break a leg, baby," he said with a wink.

Then he turned and allowed Luke and his buddy to follow him all the way to the front door.

With Luke watching closely, Vaughn walked along the side of the building toward the lesser-used street that Sydney had told him about. He glanced at it sideways as he passed and noticed that there were no cars parked anywhere near the door at the back of the building. The street, in fact, looked entirely deserted. At the far end he could see traffic passing along the perpendicular road. He kept walking and turned right down the next side street, knowing that he was being closely monitored.

"Shotgun, this is Phoenix," Sydney said in his ear. "State your position."

"I'm about a block away from the target, taking a little detour," Vaughn said. The side street was relatively quiet. He walked by stores with graffiti-covered metal gates pulled over their windows. A pair of friends chatted as they emerged from the front door of a small apartment building, heading out for the night. "Mr. Clean and his bouncer friends are going to be keeping an eye out for me, so I'm going to approach from the north end of the street, just to be safe," Vaughn said quietly, trying to avoid being noticed.

"Copy that," Sydney said. "So . . . you kissed my sister."

Vaughn laughed. "Caught that, did you?"

"How could I miss it?" Sydney asked lightly. "I *am* seeing the world through your eyes right now."

"Well, I didn't enjoy it for a second," Vaughn said, turning right at the next corner. Cars zoomed down the well-lit street. "No offense, but your sister's lips are about as soft as granite."

"None taken," Sydney said.

Vaughn could hear the smile in her voice. Whatever the mission, it was always nice having Sydney in his ear.

Finally Vaughn came to the far end of the tiny

street that ran along the back of The Moxie Club. Farther along, he could see the north end of the building and three separate loading docks, all of which were closed. Pausing, he took another survey of the street. Everything was dark and quiet. He pulled out the key card, shed his colorful jacket, and shoved it into a nearby garbage can.

"Okay, Phoenix, all's clear," Vaughn said. "I'm going in."

"Be careful," Sydney said.

"Always," he replied.

Vaughn passed by a set of Dumpsters near the corner and, as a precaution, stayed close to the wall on his approach. He reached the door and slid the key card through the slot, holding his breath. For a split second nothing happened, and he was sure that he had swiped the card the wrong way and that any moment the entire street was going to be flooded with alarms and flashing lights. But then there was a soft buzzing sound. Vaughn tried the handle, and the door swung toward him.

Inside, Vaughn looked left and right. He had entered a cavernous, two-story room filled with huge silver vats, whirring machinery, and pipes that ran in every direction. The air was warm and humid and smelled sugary sweet. Vaughn stepped inside and let the door close quietly behind him. His camera glasses instantly fogged up.

"Phoenix, I'm removing the camera," Vaughn whispered. "It's too foggy in here."

"Copy that, Shotgun," Sydney replied.

Vaughn hooked the glasses on the pocket of his pants and glanced around. From where he stood, the room seemed to be devoid of people, but one never knew.

What is this place? Vaughn thought, turning left and moving along the wall, toward the loading docks he had noticed just moments ago. Whatever Land was using his extra space for, it was nothing like The Moxie Club. On the other side of the far wall, women strutted their stuff as partyers got drunk and crammed money into G-strings. In this room, there was definitely some kind of manufacturing going on. Something that required a lot of sugar, from the scent of things.

Vaughn stopped suddenly when he heard a pair of voices. The words were too muffled by the noise of the machinery to understand, but he could tell they were coming from a small office that had been built against the wall, straight ahead. There was a tiny window cut into the side of the office. Vaughn approached silently and pressed his back against the wall next to the window.

"Everything is right on schedule," a gruff voice said. "Tell Mr. Land he has nothing to worry about."

Vaughn inched over to the window and quickly peeked inside. Two men in lab coats stood in the center of the small, cluttered office, talking urgently. One of the men was tall and broad, with thick glasses, the other a skinny blond man with slicked-back hair. Vaughn had no doubt that these were the men Sydney had seen in the alley the night before. She had e-mailed their pictures to HQ, but the database had come up blank.

"As soon as we get the vials, we can have the food prepared for delivery within hours," the man in the glasses said.

"Good," the smaller man replied with a nod. "Mr. Land will be very pleased."

"I just hope this Bergin delivers," the first man said. "We only have one chance to make this work."

Vaughn's breath caught in his throat. Whatever food they were making here, Land and his goons were planning on contaminating it with the VX411.

But what, exactly, were they manufacturing, and where did they plan to distribute it?

What's your endgame, Land? Vaughn wondered.

At that moment, one of the loading dock doors clanged and shuddered and slowly began to roll up. Outside, on the street, a truck beeped as it backed toward the opening. The men in the office turned and headed out a few feet from Vaughn's hiding place. He inched to the corner of the boxlike office and glanced around.

A large white truck was slowly entering the warehouse while the two men in lab coats looked on. As the logo on the side of the truck slowly came into view, Vaughn's eyes widened. Painted on the truck was a huge soccer ball under the words SOCCER CITY.

"Oh, my God," Vaughn said under his breath.

Soccer City was among the biggest soccer stadiums on the African continent. It could hold more than ninety thousand spectators. It was also one of the many venues to which Land Foods supplied concessions and supplies. Vaughn's knees actually felt weak. Land was planning on infecting the stadium's food with this horrific virus. He could kill thousands upon thousands of people. And according to his little friends, the food would be ready within hours. This guy was even more psychotic than they had thought.

CHAPTER 9

"Oh, my God," Vaughn said over the receiver in Sydney's ear.

"What is it?" Sydney asked, sitting forward. She automatically reopened the window that showed the feed from Vaughn's glasses, but all she could see through the condensation on the lenses was a white wall. "Shotgun, talk to me. What's going on?"

There was a shout and a scuffle. Sydney's speakers crackled and someone yelled, but she couldn't make out the words or the voice over the interference. Sydney pushed herself out of the chair, grasping the edge of the desk.

"Shotgun? Are you there?" she shouted, trying to make sense of what she was hearing. "Vaughn!"

Why the hell did you take off those glasses? she thought, desperately watching the screen for some clue as to what was going on. The image bounced around, focusing on a pair of legs, the floor, the ceiling. Suddenly the screen went blurry, and then, with a flash, went blank. Sydney could hardly breathe. Moments later, the feed came to life again, long enough for Sydney to see, through the mist on the lenses, a pair of feet being dragged in front of the camera lens. She was almost certain she recognized Vaughn's boots.

Her heart went cold. "Shotgun! Shotgun, if you can hear me, cough once."

There was nothing. Vaughn had been knocked out, and Land's men were taking him somewhere. Sydney hit a button on her computer, patching her comm through to Nadia.

"Evergreen, Shotgun has been compromised and taken prisoner, do you copy?" Sydney said, clutching her arms around her waist as she paced in front of the computer. The image was steady now, showing the corner of a piece of metal furniture through the fog. The glasses had obviously been kicked aside.

"Evergreen?" Where the hell *was* she?

There was a brief pause, and then Nadia whispered a reply. "I copy. I heard it all."

"You have to go find him," Sydney said. "Find out what happened."

Another pause. "I'm about to go out on stage," Nadia said. "Land is in the front row. He wanted to see how the crowd responded to the new girls. If I run out of here now, he'll get suspicious."

"I don't give a damn about Land right now. Vaughn is in trouble," Sydney snapped. "Claim stage fright or something."

"I'll only be on stage for three minutes," Nadia told her. "I will find him the second I'm done. I promise."

There was a high-pitched squeak on the line, and Sydney blinked, taken aback. "Nadia?" she called. "Nadia?"

She turned off her comm, Sydney realized, a blind rage overcoming her. *She's blatantly ignoring me. Who the hell does she think she is?*

Sydney ripped the earpiece from her ear and

dialed Sloane on the speakerphone, fuming. He picked up right away.

"This is Sloane," he said.

"Vaughn has been captured, and Nadia has gone rogue," Sydney said as she strapped her ankle holster on. Her pulse was racing so fast, she could hardly see straight. "I'm going after Vaughn."

"Sydney, you can't do that," Sloane said.

"This is just a courtesy call," Sydney replied tersely, trying to control her panicked breathing. "I'm not asking your permission."

"Yes, you are, whether you realize it or not," Sloane said. "Otherwise, you wouldn't have bothered calling me at all. Sydney, you know that if you're spotted anywhere near The Moxie Club, Land will know that Vaughn is an agent. Right now, he could be anyone. As soon as his affiliation is revealed, his life is as good as over."

Sydney paused for a split second, realizing the truth of this statement. But there was no way around it. She had to go to the club.

"We can't wait for Nadia to take her curtain call," she said. "Who knows what they will have done to Vaughn by then."

"Sydney, Nadia is Vaughn's field partner for

this mission," Sloane said calmly, firmly. "She will take care of it. Now I'm ordering you to stand down."

Trying not to think about the consequences, Sydney reached out and hit the speaker button on the phone, cutting Sloane off the same way Nadia had silenced her. Once again, she was on her own.

Nadia rushed backstage after her performance and grabbed a silk robe hanging on a hook near one of the makeup stations. She slipped it on over her half-naked body and sidestepped a girl stretching on the floor. The dressing room was a flurry of activity. Cigarette smoke filled the air; girls exchanged lipsticks and read magazines, waiting to go on. As Nadia grabbed her leather bag and pulled out her clothes, a feather boa whipped her in the face and left some of its faux plumage stuck to her lips.

"Nice moves, new girl," a buxom blonde said in a thick Russian accent, flopping into the makeup chair next to Nadia.

"Thank you," Nadia said quickly as she picked the feathers from her face.

She stood up and stepped into her dress, pulling it on under her robe, all the while checking the dressing room for anyone who could be of use to her. Nadia had to get to Vaughn, but in order to do that, she was going to need one of those precious key cards. Her best bet, she knew, would be to find one of Land's bouncers or bodyguards and distract him long enough to lift his card.

A couple of the girls stepped aside to let a tall, black man with a 1990s flattop make his way through the room. His eyes were trained directly on Nadia's reflection in the makeup station's mirror.

"Looks like Zeke wants to congratulate you, also," the Russian woman said, lifting her chin at the visitor. "Good for you."

Nadia caught Zeke's eye in the mirror and gave him a sexy smile. Apparently she wasn't going to have to search for one of Land's men. He was coming to her.

"Evening, Paulina," he said to the Russian.

"Zeke," she said with a knowing smile. She vacated her chair to give him more room and winked at Nadia as she sauntered away.

"You're one of the new girls," Zeke said to Nadia, leaning back against the makeup table. His voice was a deep baritone that sent reverberations through Nadia's bones. He crossed his arms and stuffed his hands under his biceps, making them look bigger than they actually were—which was rather large, anyway. "I'm Ezekiel. The girls call me Zeke."

"Aurora," Nadia said, pushing her foot into her shoe. Her hair spilled over her chest as she leaned down to use her finger as a shoe horn. Zeke seized the opportunity to take a good, long survey of her body.

"You were amazing out there, Aurora," he said. "Especially for a virgin."

Nadia made a confused face, then faked realization. "Virgin, first-timer—I get it," she said with a small laugh. She bent over again to put on her second shoe and leaned forward even farther as she did so. Looking up through her eyelashes she spotted Ezekiel's key card. It was clipped to a chain that hung from one of his belt loops. Nadia pulled on her shoe and stood up.

"In a rush to get somewhere, Aurora?" Ezekiel drawled.

"I promised my boyfriend I would call him and let him know how my first performance went," Nadia said, swinging her hair over her shoulder. "I thought I would go outside. I don't think he'll be able to hear me if I call him from in here," she added, glancing around at the noisy, gossiping ladies.

"Boyfriend, huh? Not much of a boyfriend if he didn't come see you work on your first night," Ezekiel said with a sneer. "I believe I could teach this boyfriend of yours a thing or two about manners."

Nadia smiled slowly. Knowing she was going to need a hiding place soon—nothing was going to be concealed inside her skintight dress—she took her coat from the rack by the wall and slipped her arms into the sleeves. Then she turned and took a step closer to Ezekiel, looking up at him seductively.

"I bet you tell all the girls that," she said.

"Only the ones who hang with deadbeats," he replied, standing up straight.

"And I suppose you would treat me far better than he ever has."

Nadia trailed one finger down Ezekiel's chest and around his back. With her other hand, she pulled her coat open slightly, giving him a perfect view of her cleavage. Ezekiel was, for a moment, mesmerized. Nadia used that moment to swiftly detach his key card from his belt chain. She slipped it into her pocket before he had recovered himself long enough to blink.

"You know I would," Ezekiel said.

"How, exactly, would you treat me better?" Nadia asked.

This question stopped the otherwise smooth Ezekiel cold. Apparently no one had ever asked him for specifics before. "Well, I . . ."

Nadia reached into her bag and pulled out her cell phone. "Why don't you think about that and then we'll talk," she said, backing toward the door. "*After* I've called my boyfriend."

"Huh?" Ezekiel said, confused.

"A girl has to keep her options open."

With that, Nadia turned and pushed through the door into the corridor. A pair of girls stood against the wall, talking in hushed tones. Nadia strutted by them at top speed, heading for the side door at the far end of the hall. The exit was marked EMERGENCY EXIT ONLY, but one of the dancers had told her that they disconnected the alarm long ago. The girls used the exit now as an alternative to walking out through the club and getting groped by the clientele. *Good thing. From Land's seat, he can see the entire space. If he sees me rushing out, he'll definitely wonder what's going on.*

Out on the street, Nadia hurried around the

less populated side of the building, tearing past three large cargo doors and making a left at the corner. As she reached the high-security entrance Vaughn had used, she reconnected her communication device.

"Phoenix, I'm on Shotgun's trail," she said.

There was no reply, but Nadia didn't dwell on that. Her top priority was finding Vaughn. She swiped the key card through the slot and walked into the factory. The first sounds she heard were male voices shouting angrily.

Nadia looked left and saw the small, square office at the far end of the room. The voices were definitely coming from inside. She shed her bulky fur coat as she crept toward the source of the commotion.

Nadia glanced through the office's window and quickly assessed the situation. Vaughn was inexpertly tied to a desk chair, with his arms behind his back. He probably would have been able to break free easily if he hadn't been knocked out. His head lolled forward, and a nasty cut on his forehead dripped blood all over his closed eye. Two men hovered next to him. When Nadia had first heard them shouting, she had assumed they were interrogating Vaughn. Now she realized they were yelling at each other.

"I told you not to knock him out!" the slimmer man shouted, getting in his partner's face. "What are we supposed to do with him now?"

"Kill him?" the other man suggested with a shrug of his massive shoulders.

"If we *kill* him, we'll never find out who he's working for," the first man said through his teeth.

Nadia rolled her eyes. These guys must have been good fighters to take Vaughn down, but between this argument and the unimpressive bondage skills, it was clear that they were just a couple of unprofessional thugs. Taking care of them would be no problem. She stepped into the office doorway and placed her hand on her hip.

"Have either of you guys seen Ezekiel?" she asked, pitching her voice up an octave.

The two men looked up, startled.

"What the hell are you doing back here?" the skinny guy demanded.

Nadia took a couple of steps into the room, fluffing her hair. "Ezekiel brought me back here. Said he was going to show me something cool, but then he went off to make a phone call and disappeared. I can't hang out here too long. I mean, look at what this humidity is doing to my hair."

"You shouldn't be here," the burly man said, glancing at Vaughn.

"What, like I've never seen a guy get worked over before?" Nadia asked. "What kind of business do you think I'm in?"

They both looked her up and down, taking in her revealing dress and stilettos, then exchanged a knowing look. The larger man smiled briefly, then fixed his face in a scowl once again and approached Nadia.

"You're leaving now," he said grasping her arm and turning her toward the door.

"All right, all right. No need to get testy!" Nadia said, tripping along.

Just before they reached the doorway, she brought back her elbow directly into the guy's gut. He doubled over, and she spun around, lifting her knee into his nose. There was a satisfying *crack,* and the man reeled back, clutching his face with both hands.

The thinner thug dove for one of the desks and yanked open a drawer. Nadia picked up a metal trashcan and hurled it at his arm just as he raised it, brandishing a small pistol. The gun skittered across the floor and smacked against the far wall. In his blind pain, the burly man backed toward his partner, who stumbled back against the wall. Nadia hit the larger guy with a roundhouse kick to his already battered face, and he slammed back into the file cabinets, flattening his scrawny partner behind him. The big guy fell, unconscious. His arms lay limp at his sides. His friend struggled to push the dead weight off of him.

"Who the hell are you people?" the skinny man spat, his face growing red.

Nadia grabbed the gun from the floor and pointed it at the man's head. "Sorry to do this," she said.

His blue eye's widened in terror, and Nadia flipped the gun in her hand and brought the butt down right into the man's temple. He was knocked out cold.

"Vaughn," Nadia said, kneeling behind the chair. "Vaughn, can you hear me? Wake up!"

Nadia quickly untied the rope that bound him to the chair, and he slumped forward slightly. She jumped up and caught him before he could fall to the floor. Struggling under his weight, she glanced around and saw a glass of water on one of the desks. She grabbed it and splashed the contents onto his face. Vaughn's eyes blinked, and the clean one opened slightly.

"Vaughn, can you stand?" Nadia asked.

Vaughn nodded slowly and attempted to push himself to his feet. He tipped forward into Nadia and leaned most of his weight against her side. She reached up and slung his arm around her shoulders, then clutched his stomach with both hands.

"Land . . . ," he said.

"Don't worry about that now," she said, holding him up. "I'm taking you to the hospital."

Grasping her partner to her side, Nadia moved as quickly as she possibly could toward the door.

Sydney sped down the street a block away from The Moxie Club and slammed on the brakes. As she jumped out of the car and closed the door, she heard a distinct *click* in her ear. Her heart stopped beating. Someone was on the comm.

"Phoenix, this is Evergreen. I have Shotgun, and we're en route to the hospital. Do you copy?"

"I copy," Sydney replied quickly. "Is he okay?"

"Alive . . . barely conscious," Nadia said. "I'll know more when I get there."

Sydney took a deep breath and pressed her hands into the top of her car. Tears of relief sprang to her eyes, but she held them back and breathed in and out. Vaughn was alive. He was safe with Nadia.

"Do you know the hospital?" Nadia asked.

"I know it," Sydney replied. For the moment, all was forgiven. The only thing that mattered was that Nadia had done her job after all. "Good work, Evergreen. I'm right behind you."

Sydney was about to get back in the car when a black van pulled around the corner and drove right by her. Sydney's eyes widened. Sitting in the front passenger seat, clutching a shiny metal case in his lap with both arms, was Dr. Lance Bergin. Sydney looked away quickly, hiding her face with her hair. At the end of the street, the van turned left, heading for The Moxie Club.

This is it. This is the transaction, Sydney thought. She raced after the van without a second thought. With Vaughn and Nadia sidelined, the plan to ambush Land and Bergin in the midst of their criminal activity had gone out the window. If she could just get to Bergin before he got to Land—if she could take him into custody—she could confiscate the VX411 and get him to tell her where the vaccine was. In five minutes, this could all be over.

Sydney tore around the corner at top speed. Up ahead, the van made a left into the small street behind The Moxie Club. Sydney figured she had about fifteen seconds before Bergin was ushered into Land's secret room and the impenetrable door locked behind him. She sprinted to the end of the street and saw the van's brake lights illuminate.

Bergin stepped shakily into the street, holding on to the metal case for dear life. Three huge body-guards emerged from the backseat through the sliding door. Along with the driver, they surrounded Bergin and hustled him toward the secure entrance. Sydney was outnumbered, but she would have to take them. For Eric's sake.

She raced toward the huddled group of men, ready to launch into battle, hoping that the element of surprise would help her take out at least one or two of them before the others realized what was going on. But then, suddenly, they all turned and shoved Bergin back into the van. Sydney saw that one of them was talking urgently into a cell phone.

"No! Stop!" Sydney shouted, going for her gun.

Now that Vaughn was safe, she didn't care who saw her anymore. Getting her hands on Bergin was her only concern.

None of the bodyguards even paused. They slammed the doors of the van and peeled away. Sydney aimed her gun at the back of the vehicle, but it was too late. They had already turned onto the street at the far end of the alley.

Sydney raced after them, hoping that somehow she could catch up with the van, but when she reached the busy road, the vehicle was nowhere in sight. One of Land's men must have tipped the driver off to Vaughn's presence. They must have known they were being watched.

Doubling over and trying to catch her breath, Sydney told herself that she had to stay calm. She had to meet up with Nadia and Vaughn and come up with a new plan. Unfortunately she didn't have a clue where to start. Their entire mission had focused around Bergin's meeting with Land, which had just been called off. Now she had no idea where Bergin was headed, and Land was clearly on the alert. It seemed that with every move APO made, they were driving one more nail into Eric Weiss's coffin.

CHAPTER 10

Sydney detested hospitals. Unfortunately, because of her line of work, she spent a lot of time walking their halls or recovering in their beds. She hated being a helpless patient, but even worse, she hated knowing that someone she loved was being treated in one of these tiny, sterile rooms. As she hustled through the ward under the anemic glow of the fluorescent lights, she had no idea what kind of condition Vaughn was in. She tried not to imagine the worst, but it wasn't easy.

What, exactly, had those men done to Vaughn?

Had they broken any bones? Was he conscious?

After everything she had seen in the past few years, she knew that these things could be part of a best-case scenario. Nadia had said he was alive but barely conscious, which could mean anything. Vaughn could have been tortured. They could have exposed him to electric shock, water torture, poison. He could be hanging on by a thread.

She paused outside room 415, took a deep breath, and pushed open the heavy door.

A thin curtain hid the room from the doorway. Sydney pushed it aside quietly and paused. On the far end of the private room, next to a long window, Nadia was helping Vaughn sit up in bed. She tenderly held his shoulder and placed a pillow behind his back. Vaughn, sporting a large, ugly bruise over his left eye, winced and then smiled his thanks. Nadia smiled back and squeezed his hand. Sydney could barely breathe.

It seemed as if Nadia was taking her place even out of the field lately.

"Hi," Sydney said, brushing aside her insecurities.

Vaughn turned to her, and his entire face lit up. Suddenly everything but Vaughn and his condition were forgotten. Besides having one arm in a sling, a gash on his forehead, and a black eye, he was otherwise fine. They had been lucky this time.

"Hey," Vaughn said, his voice tired. "You got here fast."

"I was at The Moxie Club when Nadia contacted me," Sydney said, crossing to his bed. She saw the look of surprise on Nadia's face when she heard where Sydney had been, but she chose to ignore it. "How are you?"

"I'm fine," Vaughn said, grimacing as he adjusted his position. "Just a sprained wrist. Nothing big. The doctors are letting me out of here in the morning."

"I'll leave you two alone," Nadia said, touching Sydney's shoulder in a comforting way as she passed by. "I'm going to call my father."

Sydney almost wanted to stop her, knowing that Sloane was going to tell Nadia about their phone call and that Nadia was going to relate Sydney's activities to her father. But they were going to hear about it sooner or later. She let Nadia go, and focused on Vaughn.

"So . . . want to talk about what you saw back there?" Sydney asked, reaching for his hand.

Vaughn's eyes were dark as he looked at her. "Syd, this guy is so much more insane than we thought. I overheard these guys talking about tainting food with the VX411. I was just trying to figure out what they were making in there when a truck pulled in through one of the loading docks."

"A truck," Sydney said.

"It was a Land Foods supply truck for Soccer City," Vaughn said. "It's a huge venue, and they're staging all these international matches there this week."

"Land mentioned that the other day when I met with him," Sydney said.

"Land Foods supplies all the concessions for the stadium," Vaughn told her. "It was in the brief Nadia and I read on the plane."

"He's going to poison the fans at one of the international matches," Sydney said, her blood running cold. "But, why? Why would he want to kill all those innocent people?"

"Who knows? This guy is obviously pathological," Vaughn said. "And now we've missed our only chance to stop the transaction."

"No, we haven't," Sydney said. "He doesn't have the virus yet."

"What?" Vaughn said, his expression brightening a bit. "How do you know?"

"I saw Bergin tonight, just before I came here," Sydney told him. "He was about to enter the factory, but his bodyguards got a call and they hustled him out of there."

"They were tipped off because of me," Vaughn said, looking away. "I can't believe this."

"At least Land doesn't have the virus yet," Sydney said. "Bergin is somewhere in Johannesburg. We can still stop him. All we have to do is find him before he gets to Land."

"How are we going to do that?" Vaughn asked.

"I don't know, but we'll find a way," Sydney told him firmly. "Once we do, this will all be over."

Sydney glanced up from her laptop screen as Nadia sat back from her own computer and crossed her arms over her chest, letting out a frustrated sigh. She looked much more like herself this morning in a simple black T-shirt and no makeup. Her long dark hair hung straight down her back.

"Lance Bergin is not listed anywhere. Not in any of the hotels or motels in Johannesburg, nor within a fifty-mile radius of the city," she said, reaching for her coffee.

"Well, I guess it was too much to hope that he was naive enough to use his real name," Sydney said, typing at her keyboard, directly across the desk from Nadia.

The two sisters were facing each other as they worked, so close that their knees were almost touching. Ever since they had gotten back to the hotel, Sydney had been waiting for Nadia to say something about her break in protocol—and to relay some scolding from Sloane—but Nadia had not brought it up once. Sydney was grateful. She would much rather be focusing on the task at hand.

"I'm going to start checking the guest lists for some kind of obvious alias," Sydney said.

She took a sip of her coffee and hit the enter button to bring up the current manifests of the three largest, most luxuriant hotels in the city. Whereas many international criminals would be smart and experienced enough to disappear in some nameless, rundown hovel, Bergin would most likely do the exact opposite. He was one of those men who had probably seen every James Bond movie and would stay in some posh place because that's what manly movie spies and slick international criminals do. A guy like him, who hardly ever left the lab, would want to make the most of his one big adventure. Sydney could tell by the way he had salivated over her and tried to seduce her by leading her to his private library that he was one science geek who was just dying to live like a rock star.

"Okay, what kind of name do you think Bergin would go for?" Vaughn asked, pacing behind Sydney. He had been released from the hospital that morning and was feeling much better after a good night's sleep and a hot shower, despite the fact that his left eye was still swollen and his right arm was secured in a blue hospital-issue sling. "He seems like the quintessential sci-fi fan to me, so . . . Luke Skywalker?" he joked.

"Captain Kirk?" Nadia added.

"Professor Xavier?" Vaughn shot back.

"Very funny," Sydney said with a smile. "And Vaughn, don't pretend that you haven't been fantasizing your whole life about wielding a light saber."

"I think Marshall has actually built one, but he refuses to confirm or deny," Vaughn said, shaking his head.

Sydney grinned. She was glad to have them both there. If she had been forced to spend one more hour in that room alone, she would have been banging her head against a wall.

Sydney slowly scrolled down the list of names with reservations at the first hotel. Nothing odd caught her eye, so she moved on to the next list. As she read, Vaughn leaned over her shoulder, bracing his good hand against the desk to her left.

"Griffin, Haagenstandt, Hogan, Huxley, Innes," Sydney read under her breath.

"Wait a minute. Go back," Vaughn said.

"What? Which one?" Sydney asked.

"Huxley," Vaughn said, pointing at the screen. "Click on that one."

Sydney clicked on the name in question, and a new window appeared with the details of the reservation and all the charges accumulated by the guest.

"A lot of room service and pay-per-view movies," Vaughn said, scanning the list of expensive breakfasts, dinners, and late-night snacks. "Sounds about right for someone lying low."

"J. Huxley checked in two nights ago . . . scheduled to leave today . . . reservation extended for one more day," Sydney read. "Sounds about right. What's the significance?"

"Julian Huxley," Vaughn explained, standing up straight. "Twentieth-century English biologist. He had all these theories on culture and evolution."

"He took the name of his favorite scientist?" Nadia said, leaning forward in her chair. "It seems a bit too easy, doesn't it?"

"No. Bergin would totally do something this prosaic," Sydney replied. "Vaughn is right. This has to be him."

"Has to be? We just started looking," Nadia protested. "Shouldn't we see if there are any other possibilities out there?"

"Are you going to fight me on this, too?" Sydney asked, her face suddenly flushing with heat.

Nadia blinked, clearly taken aback. "What else have I fought you on?"

"Last night at the club, when you refused to go after Vaughn," Sydney said.

"Sydney, this isn't about you and me," Nadia said with infuriating calm. "I'm just trying to make sure we follow all the leads."

"Well, right now, this is the only lead we have to follow, and we don't have time to sit around looking for another option that might not even exist," Sydney said, her words clipped. "Besides, the dates perfectly match up on this reservation. My gut says this is our guy."

"Your gut is not *always* right," Nadia said, lifting her shoulders.

Sydney's eyes flashed. Nadia had no idea how many times her instincts had gotten her out of life-threatening situations, how many times they had helped her beat impossible odds.

"Sydney, I'm sorry. I just think if we—"

"Fine, if you don't want to go with my gut, then I'll check it out alone," Sydney said, getting up and heading for the closet. Vaughn practically tripped getting out of her way. Sydney felt her frustration growing and struggled to keep it under control.

"Why are you getting so angry?" Nadia asked, standing as well. "If you would just—"

Sydney yanked her jacket off the hanger. She knew she was a little on edge—about Weiss, about her mistakes, about Nadia taking her place on the mission—about a lot of things. But having people point out how she was letting her emotions get the best of her only made her feel worse. Especially when the person pointing it out was Nadia. Considering how competitive she had been feeling lately, Nadia exposing her faults was about as pleasant as torture.

"I swear, if one more person tells me to calm down—"

"Whoa, you guys. Hold on," Vaughn said, stepping into the center of the room and effectively getting between them. "You're both right."

"What?" Sydney and Nadia said in unison.

"Nadia has a point. There *is* a chance that Huxley is not Bergin—that it's just a coincidence," Vaughn said. "Maybe there is a Skywalker out there somewhere," he said, bringing a bit of a smile to Nadia's face. "But Sydney's also right. We don't have time to keep searching in vain if Huxley *is* our man."

Now it was Sydney's turn to feel smug.

"Weiss's life depends on us, and we are quickly running out of second chances," Vaughn added.

Sydney took a deep breath, and Nadia looked at the floor. "You're right," Nadia said. "What's our next move?"

"I suggest the two of you go check this guy out

while I stay here and keep looking for any other suspicious names at the other hotels," Vaughn said. "I'll call you if I have any other leads. If Huxley turns out to be a dead end, you two will already be out in the field and you can check them out."

Sydney glanced at Nadia. Her eyes were flat as she stared back.

"Fine," Sydney said finally, putting on her jacket.

"Fine," Nadia repeated.

Together, they headed for the door.

"Just try not to bite each other's heads off while you're out there," Vaughn said with a small smile.

Sydney and Nadia both rolled their eyes and let the door slam behind them on their way out.

Sydney and Nadia took the elevator to the eighth floor of the Oasis Hotel, which was located right in the center of Johannesburg's retail district. As Sydney predicted, the place was like something right out of a Bond movie. The lobby was lavishly decorated with vaulted ceilings and large, flourishing potted plants placed at the end of each of the couches and divans in the waiting area. Men and women in gold vests and dark blue jackets stood behind the reception desk, their postures perfect and welcoming smiles glued on their faces. Even the elevator was beautiful, and the music playing softly through the speakers was a soothing classical tune.

Unfortunately, the lilting sound of the violin did nothing to uncoil the taut muscles in Sydney's shoulders. She and Nadia had not spoken much since they had left Vaughn behind. There were about a million things Sydney wanted to say to her sister, but right now did not seem like the time to have a heart-to-heart. From the corner of her eye she saw Nadia look at her quizzically, but she ignored it. They could address their issues later. For now, they had a job to do.

The elevator *pinged* and stopped, and the doors slid open. Sydney and Nadia stepped out into a hushed hallway. A small gold sign pointed the way to guest rooms numbered 801-812. The arrow directed them to the right, where the hallway took an abrupt turn.

Nadia glanced at Sydney, and Sydney nodded at her to go ahead. Nadia checked around the corner, then pulled quickly back.

"It looks like you and Vaughn were right," she

whispered. "There are two guards stationed outside one of the rooms."

"Land must have sent his men to protect Bergin," Sydney whispered back. "Okay. Follow my lead."

Nadia opened her mouth—perhaps to protest—then changed her mind and simply nodded. The moment she and Sydney entered the main corridor, Sydney raised her voice and started berating her sister.

"I just don't understand why you have to flirt with every girl in the room," Sydney said. "You're supposed to be in love with me."

If Nadia was taken by surprise by Sydney's tack, she didn't show it. She picked right up on the plan and immediately got into character.

"I do love you, baby," she said, reaching out to touch Sydney's face. "You're the most beautiful woman in any room."

Sydney saw the guards exchange a pleased glance. If anyone else were walking down the hall, undoubtedly the thugs would be going for their holsters right now, and they would be on full alert. But men were beyond predictable. Beautiful women always distracted them. Catfights were a huge draw, but an argument between two gorgeous lesbian lovers? Forget about it. Within seconds, the guards' eyes were riveted on the two stunning brunettes walking toward them. They were practically salivating either for a blowout, a makeup kiss, or both.

"Don't try to sweet-talk me," Sydney said, moving Nadia's hand away as they passed by Bergin's room and their captive audience. "After everything we did last night. All the things you said to me when we were in bed . . ."

Nadia paused just feet away from the guards. "I meant those things," she said, cupping Sydney's face with both hands and looking deep into her eyes. "All of those things. Every last word."

Sydney looked down, totally playing it up. She could hear the guards' heavy breathing. "Really?" she said, biting her lip.

"You know I did," Nadia said.

Then she moved in for the kiss. The guards leaned forward. Their eyes were wide.

And at the very last second, Nadia and Sydney sprang apart and attacked.

Sydney grabbed the arm of the nearest guard and slung him across the hallway, face-first into the wall. He bounced back toward her and she crouched down, causing him to flip over her back and land headfirst on the floor; as he struggled to get up, Nadia's man tripped forward into him, helped by Nadia's solid kick to his lower backbone. As the two heavyset men struggled to push each other up and away, Sydney whipped out her tranquilizer gun and shot them both at close range—one in the back of the neck, the other in his quite ample behind. They both slumped back down, out cold.

"Nice work," Nadia said, bending down and searching through the top man's pockets.

"You too," Sydney replied as she shoved the gun back into her waistband and covered it with her shirt.

Nadia came up with the electronic key to Bergin's room and flashed it at Sydney. "Let's do this."

Inside the room, they found Bergin nervously shoving clothes and food into an open suitcase on the bed. He dropped everything and raised his hands the second they walked in.

"Don't kill me," he said, his face red and damp with sweat. "Please don't kill me."

"I guess you heard us coming," Sydney replied.

His eyes widened when he got a look at her. "It's you again," he said. "I thought you were blond."

"I wasn't having more fun," Sydney said as Nadia checked the closet and bathroom for Bergin's silver case and to make sure there weren't any more guards lurking nearby. She walked back into the bedroom and shook her head.

"Where's the VX411?" Sydney asked Bergin, who was still standing, trembling with fear, with his hands raised above his head. He looked like he was about to either burst into tears or wet his pants at any second.

"You're too late," he said, his lips quivering. "Land sent one of his men to pick it up this morning."

Sydney felt everything inside of her turn to ice. She and Nadia exchanged a look of horror. "Too late." The two most awful two words an agent could hear.

"What about the vaccine?" Sydney asked him. "Where did you hide the vaccine?"

"The vaccine?" Bergin repeated.

"Yes. You exposed one of our agents to your little concoction," Nadia said, advancing on him. "We need the vaccine to save him."

Bergin's eyes widened even farther.

"So where the hell is it?" Sydney asked, her voice deadly calm.

Bergin looked from one woman to the other, wondering if there was any way out of this.

"I . . ."

At that moment, the door behind Sydney burst open, ripping the doorjamb to shreds and showering the room with splintered wood. Sydney momentarily held up her hands to shield her face and by the time she had brought them down again, one of four intruders had grabbed Bergin by the collar like a puppy and dragged him out of the room.

Oh, no way, Sydney thought. *Not again!*

She whirled around and threw a punch only to have her arm blocked by a man she dimly recognized, a goateed bodyguard—one of the four who were ushering Bergin around the night before. He backhanded Sydney across the face and she hit the floor, her eye exploding in pain. He leaned over her as she sat up, and she grabbed his collar with both hands and yanked him toward her, slamming his forehead into the top edge of the dresser behind her. He reeled back, and she took hold of his ankles, pulling him off of his feet. Her attacker fell to the floor and she jumped up, side kicking him square across the jaw. With a loud *crack,* his head jerked to the side and he stopped moving.

Sydney couldn't tell if he was knocked out or dead, but a moment later, another man grabbed her from behind, pinning both her arms down. Sydney threw her legs up and walked them up the wall, arching her back until she had flipped over the guy's shoulder and landed feetfirst on the bed. She grabbed a ceramic lamp off of the bedside table, ripped the chord from the wall, and swung with all her might, meeting the guy's face as soon as he turned around. Two of his teeth went flying from his mouth as his lip split wide open. He fell in a heap next to his already battered friend.

Sydney jumped down from the bed and was about to help Nadia with the third thug, when the fourth, who had dragged Bergin out, reappeared, gun already drawn.

"Don't even think about moving," he said, his dark eyes glowing with rage. He had a nasty red scar that ran from his temple all the way down to the corner of his mouth.

Sydney glanced left and saw that somehow the third man had pulled a gun on Nadia as well.

"On the floor. Facedown," the man with the scar said, pointing with his gun.

Sydney and Nadia, hands raised, both dropped to their knees. The disfigured thug kicked Sydney in the back, and she slammed her face against the floor. Nadia lay down before he had a chance to do the same to her.

"The van's waiting downstairs," he said to his one conscious friend. "Get going."

"You sure?" the other guy asked, out of breath.

"I got this," the scarred one said.

Sydney watched the man retreat from the corner of her eye. Big mistake. One jerk with a gun was a lot easier to take out than two. This guy clearly didn't know who he was dealing with. Had he failed to notice that they had already taken out four of his friends?

"Don't turn around!" he shouted at Nadia.

He grabbed her by the hair, drew her head back, slammed her face down into the floor, then quickly trained his gun at the back of Sydney's head before she could move.

"Don't even think about it, miss," he said, taking a step back and standing over them both. Nadia let out a groan of pain. "You move one muscle and

I won't let you decide which of you gets to see the other one die."

There was a *click* as the safety on the gun was released. He let out an evil, amused laugh. Sydney looked into her sister's eyes. They knew what they had to do.

"Now," Sydney mouthed.

In one swift motion, Nadia flipped over, locking her ankles around their captor's shin and knocking him off his feet. The gun fired as his arm flailed into the air and a mirror across the room exploded into a million tiny shards. The man slammed into the floorboards and his gun slid across the freshly waxed wood and under a dresser in the corner. As Nadia began to push herself up, Sydney dove over the man's prone body and reached for the gun. As she was spinning around, she saw him yank another pistol out of an ankle holster. Lying on his back, he straightened his arm and took aim at Nadia.

For a moment, time seemed to stop. Nadia froze as she stared down the barrel of the pistol. The man's finger curled around the trigger. There was no oxygen in the room.

Time resumed as Sydney shot the man dead with

one bullet, right through the temple. He crumpled to the floor at Nadia's feet.

Nadia gasped for breath. For a split second, neither one of them moved. Sydney had seen her own life flashing before her eyes as her sister faced down death.

"Are you okay?" she said finally, pushing herself to her feet.

"I think so," Nadia said.

Sydney put out her hand and pulled Nadia up. "Come on," Sydney said. "We can still catch up with Bergin."

Nadia tore her eyes away from the man who had almost killed her, and nodded. They both took off, tearing down the stairs, jumping down half-flights. They reached the lobby and dodged the posh guests with their tiny dogs and their rolling suitcases, drawing gasps and admonishments along the way. Sydney shoved through the gilded glass door at the far end of the lobby and skidded onto the sidewalk, with Nadia right on her heels.

They were just in time to see the familiar black van skid through a red light and disappear into traffic.

CHAPTER 11

Vaughn was just hanging up the phone when Sydney and Nadia returned from Bergin's hotel. His face was taut, and his skin was waxy and pale. Sydney took one look at him and stopped in her tracks.

"Vaughn? What is it?" she asked.

Don't let it be Weiss. Please don't let it be Weiss, she thought.

"It's Weiss," Vaughn said, swallowing hard. "He's . . . fallen into a coma."

Sydney's heart thumped faster as she looked at

Nadia. A coma. This was not good. *But at least he's still alive.*

"They think he has maybe twenty-four hours, give or take," Vaughn said, lowering himself onto the couch near the window. He ran a hand over his face and stared sorrowfully at the floor.

"Don't worry. We'll figure something out," Sydney said, sitting next to him. She touched his back gently and he looked at her, his helplessness reflected in his eyes.

"I just got off the phone with Sloane," he told her. "He says our first priority is stopping Land. We have to keep him from putting the VX411 into play."

"Agreed. But what about the vaccine?" Nadia asked.

"He says they're working on it there," Vaughn replied. "We're to focus on the terrorist threat. According to what I heard last night, the infected supplies for Soccer City should be ready to go within the next couple of hours."

"We have to get down to The Moxie Club and stop them," Sydney said.

"And if we can grab Land as well, he should be able to tell us where Bergin is," Nadia added.

"Wait a second," Vaughn said as Sydney stood.

"Sloane didn't say anything about interrogating Land. We have to stop the trucks. That is our primary objective. If you guys focus on capturing Land . . ."

"We can do both," Nadia told him firmly.

Vaughn stood up and leveled them both with a serious stare. "If we mess this up again, thousands of lives will be at stake. Weiss wouldn't want you risking all those innocent people for him."

"I can't believe you're saying this," Sydney said, her jaw dropping.

"Syd, I want to save Eric's life as much as you do," Vaughn said. "Probably more, but we have to do what we have to do."

"Exactly," Sydney said. "And what we have to do is stop the trucks *and* bring Land in."

"He's our only link to Bergin," Nadia added. "Forget what my father did or didn't say. Tonight, we kill two birds with one stone."

Sydney smiled as her sister turned and headed for the door. For the first time on this hellish mission, the two of them agreed on something.

Nadia pulled the car up to the corner diagonally across from The Moxie Club's entrance—the very same corner Sydney had lingered on the first night she checked out the club. She cut the engine and killed the lights. The same large, rowdy crowd that had been waiting to get through the door the last several nights was already lined up along the side of the building.

"I don't understand why we're not just going in through the side door," Nadia said, removing her seat belt.

"They know we got in with a key card," Sydney told her. "They've had almost twenty-four hours to change the security system. If we go anywhere near that door, we're dead. Our best bet is to go in through the front like anyone else and try to find a way into the factory through there."

"Maybe one of the other dancers has seen something," Nadia said with a nod. "I'll see what I can find out once I get backstage."

Nadia opened the door and started to climb out of the car, but Sydney stopped her, grabbing her arm.

"Hang on a sec," she said. "There's something weird here."

There were several more bouncers patrolling the area than usual. The other night there had only been two men stationed at the door to check IDs. Now she counted at least six, two of whom paced the red ropes, checking out the patrons. Another two seemed to be scanning the people passing by.

Nadia closed the car door and sat back. "They're looking for someone," she said, reading Sydney's thoughts.

One of the men at the door held up a picture next to a waiting woman's face, then shook his head and let her pass through. Sydney felt a wave of fear. She pulled out a pair of tiny, high-tech binoculars and trained them on the bouncer.

"What is it?" Nadia asked, shifting in her seat.

Sydney adjusted the focus and zoomed in on the bouncer's hand. He flipped the picture over and showed it to the guy next to him. Sydney was able to see the image clearly, and her heart sunk.

"It's a picture of Vaughn . . . and of you," Sydney said, handing the binoculars over. "I don't know why I'm surprised. Once they figured out who Vaughn was, of course they would suspect you as well."

"I don't believe it," Nadia said, staring through the lenses. "Where did they get that photograph?"

"They probably have security cameras all over the club," Sydney said.

"Every one of those bouncers has my picture," Nadia said, lowering the binoculars. She smirked. "I guess I don't get any stage time tonight."

"You'll have to stay here," Sydney told her, reaching for the door.

"Sydney, you can't go in there alone," Nadia said. "Land must have two dozen men both inside and out. Are you going to take them all on yourself?"

I've seen worse odds, Sydney thought.

"We don't have much of a choice," Sydney said. "You step one foot near that place and they're going to be all over you."

Nadia sighed and desperately scanned the scene. Sydney knew exactly how she felt. Helpless, useless, sidelined.

"Fine," she said finally. "But stay in contact with me. Keep me informed. If I don't hear from you, I'm coming after you."

"I will," Sydney said, stepping out of the car and slamming the door. She was about to head across the street to talk the bouncers into letting her cut the line, when Nadia lowered the passenger side window.

"Sydney! Get down!" she hissed.

Sydney instantly dropped to the sidewalk, her heart pounding. Her bare palms pressed against the cool asphalt, still damp from an earlier sun shower.

"What is it?" she whispered.

"Land. He just came out the front door," Nadia replied.

Sydney lifted her head slightly and peeked over the car. Sure enough, Peter Land himself was standing near the entrance, consulting with the bouncers. They looked at the picture, and Land patted one of the men on the back, telling him to keep up the good work. Then he walked down the few steps to the sidewalk and made a right, heading toward the side street that led to his factory.

"What's he doing?" Nadia asked.

"I don't know, but I'm following him," Sydney said, standing. "If I can grab him now, we can get all the answers we need."

"Be careful," Nadia said solemnly.

"Don't worry," Sydney replied.

She took off across the street and hurried after Land. A couple of the bouncers checked her out as she passed—she did bear a certain resemblance to her sister—but they realized she wasn't their mark and didn't bother her. Land turned right onto the side street, and Sydney hurried after him. She drew her gun just as he reached the security door.

"Stop right there and put your hands over your head," she said, training the gun on his chest and stepping toward him.

Slowly, Land turned around, a knowing smile stretching across his features.

"Why, Miss Bristow," he said pleasantly, placing his hands casually into his pockets. "Are you still in town? What a nice surprise."

"Hands up," Sydney said, irritated by his nonchalance. Something was not right here.

At that moment, no less than ten men emerged from the shadows. Sydney's heart slammed into her rib cage. She was surrounded, and each of the men had a pistol directed right at her.

"I believe it's you who should have her hands up," Land said, stepping toward her as the men closed in. "You should have left well enough alone, Sydney." His face was just inches from hers now. "I find it so distasteful when my friends get in my way."

"Drop the gun," one of the men said, his voice gruff. "Do it now."

Seething with anger, Sydney raised her hands. She glared defiantly at Land as she let her gun clatter to the ground. There was nothing she could do in the face of ten armed guards, but she was not going to show any weakness in front of this bastard.

"Thank you for your cooperation," Land said.

A moment later Sydney felt a crushing pain in the back of her skull, and then everything went black.

Nadia drummed her fingers against the center console as she stared out the window.

Talk to me, Sydney, she thought. *Just say something.*

She blew out an exasperated sigh and gripped the steering wheel with both hands. There was nothing good about this situation. Nadia didn't like the fact that Sydney had been forced to go in alone. She didn't like the fact that she was stuck in the car. And she especially didn't like the tense vibe that had been radiating between herself and her sister for the last day or so. Sydney seemed to take everything Nadia said the wrong way. Sometimes it was like she was disagreeing with her just to disagree. That kind of attitude was never going to work in the field.

The moments ticked by in silence. Nadia checked her watch. Sydney should have updated her by now. Nadia turned on her mic and hoped the sinking feeling in her stomach would amount to nothing.

"Phoenix, this is Evergreen, do you copy?" she asked.

Nothing but dead air.

"Phoenix, I repeat, what's your position?" Nadia demanded.

Again, nothing. There was no doubt in Nadia's mind that Sydney could take Land. Easily. Something must have happened to her in that alleyway. Something she was unprepared for.

Nadia scanned the crowded sidewalk in front of The Moxie Club. The bouncers were still looking for her. She was going to have to find some other way into the building. But how? All the entrances were covered. Without a helicopter and a skylight, she was out of options.

Wait a minute . . . the roof, Nadia thought, her eyes looking skyward. With all the pipes and machines in the factory, there had to be some kind of upper-level ventilation. She was about to call Vaughn to have him check the schematics of the building on his computer, but she stopped herself. She didn't want to let him know that Sydney was in trouble just yet, in case he decided to rush down here like a madman just like Sydney had when Vaughn was caught. She hit Marshall's button on her speed dial instead.

"This is Marshall," he said.

"Marshall, it's Nadia."

"Oh, hey! How's it going over there?" he asked.

"Not so good. I need you to check the satellite pictures of The Moxie Club," Nadia said. "Is there any roof access?"

She could hear him clicking away at his computer keyboard. "Looks like there's a row of five large skylights on the west side of the building," Marshall said. "The factory side."

"Perfect. Thanks, Marshall," Nadia said. She hung up the phone before he could ask her any questions. She didn't want APO to know what was going on until she had the situation under control.

Taking a deep breath, Nadia slammed the car into gear and sped through the intersection, passing The Moxie Club's line on her left. She turned left at the next corner and slowed as she passed the cargo doors, looking to see if there was any activity. Everything was still. She made another left into the now familiar alleyway with the locked entrance and cut the lights. For a split second, Nadia was dizzy with dread. There was no one in sight. Sydney and Land were both gone.

For about ten seconds while she was driving around the building, Nadia had been forced to take her eyes off of the alley's exit. Sydney could be anywhere right now if Land had decided to remove her from the premises.

Nadia resolved not to think about that. She got out of the car and jogged over to a Dumpster near the corner of the building. A slim pipe ran up the wall and hooked over the roof. It didn't look very sturdy and wasn't much to hang on to, but it was the only option she had. Nadia climbed on top of the Dumpster and dusted her hands off on her thighs.

"Shotgun, this is Evergreen," she said, activating her microphone.

"What's going on, Evergreen?" Vaughn asked in her ear.

"Phoenix has been captured," Nadia said. "I'm going in after her."

"What?" Vaughn blurted.

"I'm going to keep the airwaves open so you can hear everything that's going on," Nadia told him calmly. "I'm headed to the roof of the factory to try to find a way in."

"I'm coming down there," Vaughn said.

Nadia's first instinct was to tell him to stay put. It seemed like whenever one of them came to The Moxie Club, everything went awry. But she knew he wouldn't be able to sit at the hotel and do nothing.

"Probably a good idea," Nadia said. "We may need a little backup."

"I'm on my way," Vaughn said.

"Copy," Nadia replied.

Tilting her head back, Nadia gauged the distance between herself and her goal. She was going to have to climb at least two stories. She just hoped the pipe's rusty clamps would hold her weight. With a deep breath, she grasped the pipe and started to climb.

One hand over the other, Nadia ascended toward the sky, shimmying up the pipe like it was a training center rope. Halfway up the wall, she heard a loud creak and her heart stopped, but it wasn't one of the clamps. She looked down and saw one of Land's many guards emerge from the factory door and light up a cigarette. If only he had done that moments ago, Nadia could have grabbed the door, knocked him out with a good jab to the nose, and gone in the easy way.

As she clung to the pipe, her muscles started to shake from the strain, and she forced herself to start climbing again. The second the guy's back was turned, Nadia raced up the last few feet to the roof and hoisted herself over the edge. She could have sworn the guy had looked skyward just as she rolled onto her back, but she was pretty sure he hadn't seen anything. Still, she lay motionless for a moment to catch her breath, and waited to hear if any alarms sounded.

After a couple of seconds of silence, Nadia pushed herself up and ran over to the skylights. They were foggy and grimy, but through the haze she could see into the factory down below. At least a dozen men and women in lab coats and hairnets packed chocolate bars into boxes, while workers in blue coveralls loaded the boxes into trucks.

Chocolate? They've mixed the VX411 into chocolate? Nadia thought. Bergin must have found a way to transform the liquid into solid form so that it could be used in recipes, but not inhaled. But why chocolate? Didn't Land know that most of those candy bars were probably going to be sold to kids at the stadium?

This bastard needed to be stopped. Nadia grasped the edges of one of the skylights and pulled, but nothing happened. It was then that she noticed that each of the metal frames had a latch, and that each one of those latches was padlocked.

What next? Nadia wondered.

There was a flurry of motion down below, and Nadia leaned forward to get a better look. Two men were carrying a body between them across the factory toward a smaller room positioned directly across from the office where Nadia had found Vaughn. The body was a limp, lifeless Sydney.

Nadia was on her feet in an instant, her adrenaline kicking into overdrive. That was her sister. She was not going to lose her. She pulled out her gun and took aim, blasting one of the padlocks to smithereens. With all the work going on down below, she was fairly certain no one would hear the noise. Either way, she was determined to get into that factory one way or another.

She quickly removed the shattered pieces of the lock. One glance through the window told her that no one had heard the gunshot. Carefully, she lifted the heavy frame and slid it aside. Now there was nowhere to go but down.

Nadia inspected the area just beneath her skylight. There was a slim chance she could drop in unnoticed behind all the workers, and that the machinery would drown out her fall. But if she dropped three stories to the floor, she would definitely break a leg, and then she wouldn't be of any help to Sydney. Then Nadia saw that just to the right of the workers was a large pile of cardboard boxes. They looked empty. If she could aim for those boxes, they would break her fall, and then all she would have to do was get up and get fighting as quickly as possible.

This is never going to work, she realized, shaking her head. But she had to try. Who knew what these guys were doing to Sydney right now while she sat up here hesitating? Taking a deep breath, Nadia slid to the opening and lowered her feet down, grasping the rim of the window with her fingers.

For a moment, she dangled there, unseen by any of the workers who were bent over their stations. She swung herself backward and forward, backward and forward, gaining momentum, her eyes trained on the pile of brown boxes.

Here goes nothing, she thought. *It's just a pile of foam like gymnasts flip into when they're training. Just a pile of foam.*

Nadia swung one last time and let go.

She plummeted through the air and slammed into the boxes, her eyes closed to shield them from corners. The pile exploded beneath her and her shoulder rammed against the floor, jarring every bone in her body.

Okay, maybe not the best idea, Nadia thought, wincing as she quickly pulled herself to her feet.

She wasn't quick enough, however. Before she could even fully stand, three guards had drawn their guns and were advancing on her from various points in the room.

"Evergreen, what's going on?" Vaughn said in her ear. "Are you okay?"

Nadia looked into the dark eyes of one of her captors. May as well let Vaughn know the mission status. She took a deep breath and put her hands over her head. "I am totally screwed," she said.

That should get the message across.

* * *

Sydney opened her eyes and looked directly into a bright white light above her head. She groaned as an explosion of pain erupted in the back of her skull. She tried to raise her hands, but they had been clamped down at her sides. From the cold penetrating through her clothing, she figured she had been strapped to some kind of metal slab. She squeezed her eyes closed and waited for the pain to subside. When she opened them again, she did so much more carefully, turning her head to the side and away from the harsh light. Her head pounded painfully whenever she so much as breathed.

Okay, just get your bearings, she told herself. *Where are you?*

Sydney inhaled a deep breath as her eyes started to focus. She recognized the sweet smell of chocolate. She could hear a lot of activity on the other side of the white wall she was now staring at—it sounded like people were bustling around, trying to complete something as quickly as possible. Dimly, she recalled Vaughn and Nadia describing the scents in Land's factory and realized she must still be there. This was a positive development. At least Nadia, Vaughn, and the rest of APO would be able to come after her.

There was a low moan off to Sydney's left, and she whipped her head around. Stabbing pains radiated out from the back of her head and down through her temples and jaw. She forgot all about her discomfort, however, when she saw her sister strapped to the table next to her. Sydney wasn't sure whether to be angry that Nadia had come after her, or relieved that she wasn't alone.

"Nadia!" Sydney whispered. "Nadia! Wake up!"

Slowly, Nadia blinked her eyes open and turned her head to face Sydney. "What happened?" she asked.

"I was hoping you could tell me," Sydney hissed. "What are you doing here? I told you to wait in the car."

"Can we do the big-sister scolding later?" Nadia asked, rolling her wrists around. "We have to find a way out of here."

Good point, Sydney thought. Moving her head as much as possible with the restraints, she surveyed her immediate area, but aside from a closed metal cabinet three feet away, she saw nothing. No phone, no computer, no desk that would contain helpful paper clips or pens—nothing.

"This place is pretty bare," Nadia said, pulling

at her leg restraints. "It's like they knew we were coming."

Sydney swallowed hard and thought back to the number of guards who had been lying in wait for her in the alleyway. Those guys had definitely known she was coming. Or, at the very least, they had been prepared for every scenario.

"Does Vaughn know you're here?" Sydney asked.

"We were on comm when they caught me," Nadia replied. "But I don't think he can take on two dozen men with a sprained wrist."

Sydney swallowed hard. Nadia was right; It wasn't 100 percent certain that Vaughn would try to find them, but if he did, it was basically a suicide mission. The situation couldn't have been more grim.

"He's putting the VX411 into candy bars," Nadia said quietly. "He's infecting the chocolate he's sending to the stadium."

Sydney digested this information, feeling like the ultimate failure. Thousands of people were going to die horrible deaths if she didn't figure out a way to get out of here.

"I can't believe I ever thought that Peter Land was a decent person," Sydney said.

The door at their feet opened, and Sydney lifted

her head, ignoring the stab of pain. She felt a surge of pure hatred as Land walked into the room.

"My guests are awake," Land said, clasping his hands at waist level and giving them a welcoming smile. He was wearing the most casual clothes Sydney had ever seen him in—tan pants and shirt along with an army green jacket. He looked like a delivery man. "I trust you're both comfortable."

Sydney said nothing. She simply regarded him with her coldest stare.

"Who knew that the U.S. government had not one, but two such beautiful agents at their disposal," Land said, strolling over to stand next to Nadia. "Of course, I'm sure they didn't realize they were actually *disposing* of you when they sent you my way, or they would have been more careful."

He reached out and gently ran his finger through Nadia's hair, pulling it out so it fanned down the side of the table. Nadia stared at the ceiling, refusing to even acknowledge him.

"You see, I'm not going to let anyone stand in the way of my revenge," Land said, looking at Sydney. "Not even you, Miss Bristow."

"Your revenge?" Sydney spat. "On thousands of innocent people? On children?"

"Collateral damage, my friend," Land said with a sneer. "The world needs to see what I am capable of. They need to know just how grave the consequences can be when a man like me is ignored."

What the hell is he talking about? Sydney wondered, looking into his eyes. "If they're collateral damage, then who is your target? Why are you doing all this?"

"Why even bother asking a question when you know you're not going to get an answer?" Land asked in a patronizing tone. "You won't be breathing much longer, you know. It's a shame to waste so much of your time and energy."

"You're psychotic. You know that, don't you?" Sydney said

Land chuckled. "That very well may be. But then, I'm standing here a free man," he said, lifting his arms. "And look where your sanity has gotten you."

Sydney looked away as he left Nadia's side and approached her. If only he hadn't tricked her that first day in his office. If only she had seen through him and taken him into custody then.

"Oh, I wish you were going to be alive to see my endgame, Miss Bristow," he said, standing next to her. "But instead, you and your lovely partner are going to find out exactly what it feels like to die of VX411."

Sydney's heart skipped a beat, and she looked up at him.

"Don't worry. You won't suffer as long as your friend back in the States," he said, causing Sydney's stomach to turn violently. "I had Dr. Bergin make me an extra-potent batch. It should take about half the normal gestation period. You'll be dead within a couple of days. But at least you'll be here for each other while you go," he added, looking from Sydney to Nadia with a smile.

"You sick bastard," Sydney said. She wanted to reach out and strangle him. Kill him for Weiss. Kill him for Nadia. Kill him for all the people who were going to suffer at his hands. But it was no use. The restraints were too tight. Sydney wasn't going anywhere.

Land turned toward the door. "Good-bye, Sydney," he said. "It's been a pleasure."

He flipped the light switch as he walked out, leaving Sydney and Nadia in complete darkness.

Marcus Dixon walked into Arvin Sloane's office, his heart pounding in his ears. Jack Bristow was in the middle of a hushed conference with Sloane, and both men looked up as Dixon made his entrance. Jack took one look at his colleague's horrified expression, and his face lost what little color it had.

"Dixon? What is it?" Jack asked.

"I've just gotten off the phone with the director of special events at Soccer City in South Africa," Dixon said, wiping a clammy hand on his jacket. "I think I've uncovered Land's target."

"Well?" Sloane prompted. "What is it?"

Dixon took a deep breath. His throat was so dry, he almost coughed. "Berg Barend, the former prime minister of the Netherlands—the very man who had Petyr Olander excommunicated—is, as we speak, on South African soil."

Jack and Sloane exchanged a look of shock.

"He is visiting the country with his grandson, Eustatius," Dixon continued.

"Eustatius Barend," Jack said. "The front-runner in the upcoming general election. The man who is almost surely going to be the next prime minister of that country."

"Exactly," Dixon said with a short nod. "They are accompanied by a group of teenagers from their homeland—the country's most promising future athletes. Tomorrow, the prime minister, his grandson, and this group of youngsters are scheduled to attend a soccer match between the South African national team and the Danish national team."

Sloane stood up slowly. Dixon was almost surprised to note that the APO director looked genuinely shocked and appalled. He would have thought that a man with a heart of stone would be void of those kinds of emotions.

"You're telling me that the Barends and these children are going to be at Soccer City tomorrow?" Sloane said.

"Yes," Dixon said.

"Gentlemen," Jack said, his mouth set in a resigned grimace, "we have our endgame."

CHAPTER 12

"At least Vaughn knows we're in trouble," Nadia said. "I got one last message to him before they took my comm device."

Sydney took a deep breath. All she wanted to do was shout at Nadia. If she had just stayed in the car like Sydney had told her to, then she could be with Vaughn right now and they could both be working on a way to stop Land *and* free Sydney. It was bad enough that Sydney had been captured, but they weren't helping anyone as long as they were both imprisoned.

"He knows, but like you said before, I don't really see what he's going to be able to do by himself," she said, fighting to keep her frustration out of her voice. She knew that fighting with Nadia now would get them nowhere.

The cold emanating from the metal table had long since seeped through her clothes, and she was starting to shiver. After spending the last hour struggling to free herself to no avail, chattering teeth was the least of her problems, but it was like adding insult to injury. She already felt helpless and impotent; now she was starting to feel weak as well.

"We have to stay positive," she said aloud, trying to rouse herself as much as Nadia. She rolled her wrists around in their restraints, the now chaffed skin stinging with pain as it rubbed against the leather band.

"Agreed," Nadia said, nodding slightly. "Maybe Vaughn will call for backup. Maybe he *can* take on all those men."

Yeah, because Vaughn is suddenly Superman, Sydney thought sarcastically. She had no doubts about his abilities as an agent. Dozens of times she had seen him survive seemingly impossible odds.

But this situation was pretty bleak. Even if Vaughn could get through the impassable security door, he wasn't going to be able to take *all* those guards by surprise. At best, he could take out half a dozen before they grabbed him as well. Then they would all be stuck in this tiny cell.

A loud rumble cut off Sydney's train of thought. She looked right, as if she could see through the wall to the factory and loading bays. Someone had just started up a truck's engine. And another. There were a few slamming doors, a couple of shouted instructions. Apparently Land's men were finished loading up the chocolate bars. The VX411-infected chocolate bars.

"Maybe he won't have to," Sydney said quietly, her heart filled with dread. The trucks were thrown into gear and slowly pulled out of the factory. Sydney held her breath until the sound of their engines mixed with the background noise of the city and finally disappeared. There was a metallic screech as the loading dock doors creaked shut, and then all was silent.

Sydney turned her head to look at her sister. Her eyes had somewhat adjusted to the darkness, and she could just make out the outline of Nadia's face in the dim light from under the door. Still, she knew they were both thinking the same thing. The virus was on its way and there was nothing they could do about it. They had failed, yet again. And now that Land's plan had been set into motion, there was no reason for him to keep Sydney and Nadia alive any longer.

"We have to get out of here," Sydney said, her heart slamming into her rib cage.

"We've tried everything," Nadia said. "The tables are bolted to the floor, and we're bolted to the tables. Land knows what he's doing."

At that moment, the door to the office opened, blinding Sydney with bright white light. Two men came in, carrying glasses of crystal-clear water. Sydney tried in vain to sit up, straining her arm muscles and tearing open the already raw skin around her wrists.

"No use struggling, miss," one of the men said, stepping up to Sydney's side. "Make this easy on yourself."

Sydney held her breath as he brought the rim of the glass toward her lips. Her pulse pounded wildly in her ears, screaming at her to get away. But all she could do was press her lips together and thrash. Her only hope was to knock the glass out of his hand. Marshall had told the agents that once the VX411 was mixed with another compound like water or food, it couldn't go airborne—it could only be ingested. Unless this stuff got into her digestive system, it would be useless.

"You're only hurting yourself here," he said, grabbing her chin between his fingers. His grip was like a vise. Sydney's eyes rolled wildly, trying to get a glimpse of Nadia. She was struggling as hard as Sydney was and, as far as Sydney could tell, had not ingested any of the poison yet.

"Come on," the man holding Sydney said, grunting from the effort of trying to hold her still. "Drink up like a good little girl."

He pressed his fingers together, forcing her lips into a pucker. Sydney clamped her jaw shut, sweating with exertion. She tried to kick her legs, struggling to free her blood-soaked hands. She wasn't going to let a nameless, faceless thug kill her. Not here. Not today.

But then, forced by muscles beyond her control, her lips started to part. Try as she might, she couldn't struggle against his grip any longer. She wanted to scream in frustration, but that would be the end of her.

Help us, she thought. *Somebody, just—*

Her mouth opened. The glass tilted toward her lips. The asshole above her was smiling.

And then, suddenly, his hand jerked. His eyes went wide. Sydney turned her head as he dropped the glass and it shattered on the concrete. His huge bulk slouched over her body, then slipped to the floor.

Slowly, carefully, Sydney turned and looked at the door. Vaughn stood there, gun still drawn, chest heaving as he caught his breath. Sydney glanced at Nadia. Her attacker was down as well. She shot a grateful look at Vaughn, and then closed her eyes in relief.

"About time," she said after she had caught her breath.

"I'm so sorry," he said, holstering his gun as he walked over to Nadia and loosened her restraints. Nadia's wrists were bloody and her dark hair was matted to her face with sweat. "This place was crawling with armed guards until a couple of minutes ago. I had no choice but to wait until they were gone."

"So how did you get in?" Sydney asked as Nadia released her ankles and Vaughn worked on her arms.

"About a dozen of the guards went with Land and the trucks," Vaughn said. "The rest were just factory workers, and I guess they've officially clocked out. The only guys left were these two and a couple of others I took out in the factory."

Sydney sat up and winced as she got a look at her hands. "So that *is* what we heard," she said. "The VX411 is on its way."

"We have to go after them," Nadia said.

"I have the van outside," Vaughn said. "You guys can get taped up in there," he told them, leading the way out. "And you can brief Sloane while I drive."

Sydney exchanged a look of dread with Nadia. "Can't wait."

Sydney held out her wrists to Nadia as the van bumped along an old street desperately in need of repaving that led out of Johannesburg. Nadia gingerly wrapped Sydney's skin in gauze and tore a piece of tape to secure it with her teeth. On a small computer screen mounted to the van's wall, Sloane briefed them on the current situation. Sydney clenched her jaw, glad to have her wounds to distract her so that she didn't have to look Sloane directly in the eye while he scolded them. Being put in her place was getting a little old.

"The South African and Dutch governments have both been notified of the threat, but former Prime Minister Barend has refused to change his plans," Sloane told them, his voice flat. "He says that he and his people will not be intimidated by terrorists."

"Are they at least adding extra security at the stadium?" Nadia asked as she finished taping up Sydney's wrist.

"Yes, and the concession stands have been closed," Sloane said. "But none of this is going to matter, because you three are going to stop those trucks before they get within five miles of that stadium."

"We're working on it," Sydney said, turning toward the screen now that she and Nadia were all cleaned up and bandaged.

"I don't want to hear that you're working on it. I want to hear that it's done," Sloane snapped. "Both the Dutch authorities and the South African authorities are already up in arms about the fact that the United States government has allowed such a dangerous weapon to leave our soil. I don't have to tell you what a huge blow it will be for our country if Land manages to use this thing to kill even one innocent person. It will be a diplomatic disaster."

"Of course," Sydney said, trying to keep her voice cool. She, Nadia, and Vaughn knew all this already. They were well aware of what was at stake.

"Now I want you to clean up this ridiculous mess you've made," Sloane said. "Destroy the infected food and take Land into custody. I don't want to hear from any of you again until this is done."

"Yes, sir," Nadia said, clearly chagrined.

The screen went blank.

"Well, that was fun," Sydney said, swinging her legs around to face front.

Vaughn glanced at her over his shoulder. "Why do you think I offered to drive?"

"This is insane," Sydney said, her frustration finally boiling over. She grabbed the two front seats and leaned forward, staring at the blackness outside the windshield. "How are we ever going to find them?"

"This is the least trafficked route to the stadium," Vaughn told her. "Land's smart enough to try to get there under the radar. We'll catch up to them, don't worry."

Sydney sat back and took a deep breath. "We shouldn't even be here," she said quietly. "We should be trying to track down Bergin and find the vaccine."

"We want to save Weiss as much as you do, Sydney," Nadia said. "But my father is right. We have to try to save these people first. Their lives, and the potential damage to the U.S., are our responsibility."

"You should have waited back at the club," Sydney told her, her eyes flashing. "You should have at least waited for Vaughn. The two of you could have stopped Land."

"I thought they were going to kill you!" Nadia protested.

"I can take care of myself," Sydney shot back irrationally.

"Right. You really proved that tonight," Nadia snapped in return. "Why is it all right for you to run in inadvisably when Vaughn is in trouble, but when I come after you it's like I've committed a sin?"

"Because I *told* you to wait," Sydney replied.

"I can't believe you!" Nadia shouted, turning in her seat. "You are such a hypocrite! I just—"

"Hey! Hey! Hey!" Vaughn shouted, practically turning around in his seat. "Can we drop this, please? You two can engage in all the sibling rivalry you want, once this mission is over, but right now I need you to focus. Thousands of lives are at stake here."

Sydney tore her eyes away from Nadia's seething glare and looked out the window. Suddenly she felt like a petulant child. Enough was enough. She had let her emotions get the best of her one too many times on this mission. It was time to let it go.

"Did you see that?" Nadia asked suddenly.

"What?" Sydney asked, sitting forward.

"There! Brake lights!" Nadia said.

Sydney's heart skipped a beat as she saw a flash of red bobbing in the pitch-black night.

"It's the trucks. It has to be," she said. "Vaughn, can this thing go any faster?"

"We're about to find out," Vaughn said, gripping the wheel with his good hand and accelerating. "Brace yourselves."

Sydney and Nadia both sat back again. Sydney

pressed her feet into the floor and her hand into the wall as Vaughn leaned on the gas pedal. The van bumped faster and faster over the rough terrain, and the lights ahead grew nearer. Finally Sydney could see the white back panel of the first truck looming against the darkness.

"I'm gonna try to run him off the road," Vaughn told them.

Fighting to keep the van steady, Vaughn pulled up alongside the truck. The driver glanced at them through the window and did a double take. He tried to speed up, but the hulking truck was no match for the van.

"Hold on!" Vaughn shouted.

The engine roared as he veered right and slammed the side of the truck. The driver swerved off the road for a moment, but got back on track. He hunched forward slightly, and Sydney saw another man leaning over the driver's back, struggling to aim a gun as the truck lurched along the road.

"Vaughn! Watch out!" Sydney shouted.

The guy fired the gun, and at the exact same moment, Vaughn cut the wheel right again, ducking his head. The bullet hit the roof of the van and ricocheted off just as Vaughn slammed the truck again. The shooter was thrown forward, and the driver lost control of the wheel. There was a loud screech of tires as the truck swerved off the road, raced head-long into a line of bushes, and toppled into the ditch that ran along the side of the gravelly pavement. The truck flipped onto its side, skidded into a tree, and burst into flames.

Sydney looked out the back window of the van as one of the men managed to climb out of the smoldering truck and race away from the wreckage. Then, everything exploded in a burst of orange and yellow flames. The reverberation shook the van, and Sydney and Nadia instinctively covered their faces. When she looked up again, all Sydney saw was smoke.

"That takes care of one load," Sydney said.

Vaughn was already chasing down the second truck. Sydney's eyes widened as it loomed a mere ten yards ahead.

"They've stopped!" she shouted.

Vaughn slammed on the brakes and cut the wheel as Land and a pair of his goons got out of the truck, guns blazing. The side of the van was peppered with bullets.

"Get down!" Vaughn shouted, ducking to the floor between the front seats.

Nadia and Sydney both hit the deck as pockmarks appeared all over the metal siding of the van. Luckily, Vaughn had thought fast enough to stop with the sliding side door facing away from the shooters. Nadia reached up and grasped the handle, ripping the door open. Sydney crawled out, taking cover behind one of the wheels, and Nadia followed. They both drew their guns.

"You ready?" Sydney asked Nadia.

"Let's finish this," Nadia replied.

Sydney steeled herself for combat and stood up, taking a couple of shots over the front of the van. Three shots fired back, hitting the windshield and the hood. Sydney ducked back behind the van. Now she knew the shooter's position. She waited three seconds, then popped up again, took aim, and shot the man right in the chest.

Back behind the van, Sydney checked on Nadia. The gunfire was constant, but she was holding her own, firing around the back of the vehicle.

"I need a better angle," Sydney said. "I'm heading for those trees."

"I'll cover you," Nadia told her.

Sydney nodded, then raced out from behind the van, shooting toward the enemy vehicle. She saw another guy go down, and a third take cover behind one of the truck's massive wheels. Land was nowhere in sight. She dove into the underbrush near the trees just as another bullet whizzed by her ear.

Without hesitation, Sydney stood up and took out the third shooter.

Where the hell is Land? Sydney thought, standing back against the trunk of a large tree. Shots were still being fired. She peeked around the side and saw Nadia take out another gunman. Then, out of nowhere, an inhuman screech split the air. Sydney turned around and saw Land emerge from the ditch on the other side of the road. His eyes were wild as he aimed right at Nadia's back.

"Nadia!" Sydney shouted at the top of her lungs.

Her sister spun around, but it was too late. Land fired, and Nadia went down.

"No!" Sydney screamed. *Not my sister!*

Her arm shaking, she tried to take aim. Land walked toward the van and stood over Nadia's prone body. Sydney's vision swam. She fired off a shot, but it missed its mark. Land lifted his gun, aiming at Nadia's skull.

Oh God, no, Sydney thought, frozen with fear. *No!*

Three shots were fired. Sydney closed her eyes and fell to her knees and heard nothing but the rushing of blood through her ears. She couldn't do this. She couldn't lose yet another person she loved.

"She's all right!" Vaughn shouted. "Sydney, she's still breathing!"

Sydney forced her eyes open. She saw Land's blood-spattered body twisted on the ground. Vaughn was crouched over Nadia. It was Vaughn who had fired the three shots—Land hadn't realized there was still an agent inside the van. Vaughn had saved her sister.

Sydney rose shakily to her feet and raced over to Nadia and Vaughn. She fell to the ground at Nadia's side, her eyes wet with tears. Nadia's body felt limp and lifeless as Sydney lifted her head into her lap. She blinked and stared blankly up at the sky.

"He hit an artery. She's losing a ton of blood," Vaughn said, wrapping Nadia's leg with a thick strip of cloth and tying it off tightly to try to stop the bleeding. "We have to get her to a hospital."

Sydney nodded through her tears. "It's going to be all right," she told her sister, touching her forehead and brushing her hair back from her face. *I'm sorry I've been so impossible,* she thought. *Just stay with me and I swear I'll never tell you what to do again.* "Nadia, do you hear me? You're going to be fine."

Nadia's eyes seemed to focus on her for a split second, and Sydney waited for her to speak. Instead, her sister closed her eyes and fell unconscious in her arms.

CHAPTER 13

Sydney sat with an open folder in her lap, staring across the plane at Nadia, who slept peacefully, her blood pressure and heart rate being monitored by small, humming machines. She couldn't believe how close she had come to losing her sister. *Her sister.* Sydney was hardly accustomed to using the phrase, and she had almost lost her.

"She's going to be all right," Vaughn said, sitting down across from Sydney. His arm was still wrapped in the bright blue sling, and he winced a little as he shifted in his seat.

"I know," Sydney replied. She picked up her pen and pretended to make a note on her report, then glanced at him for a moment and tried to smile. "This has been a long week."

"Tell me about it," Vaughn said. "But at least we destroyed all the VX411. The soccer match went off without a hitch, and we took out a major threat to international security."

"I just wish we could have brought Land in alive," Sydney said. "I know you did what you had to do to save Nadia, and believe me, I'm grateful, but—"

"Now we're back at square one, as far as Weiss is concerned," Vaughn finished for her.

"Exactly," Sydney said.

She looked out the window to her left, at the bright blue sky and the fluffy clouds below. According to Marshall, Weiss had been in a coma for twenty-four hours now. His vitals were stable at the moment, but the doctors had no idea how long he might have to live.

"Bergin is out there somewhere with the answer," Sydney said. "How the hell are we going to find him?"

"I have no idea," Vaughn replied. He rubbed his free hand over his face, scratching his palm

over the stubble that covered his chin. He looked
tired and worried and haggard. "But we will find
him," he said, sounding far more confident than he
appeared. "He's just one man. A weak scientist
and a rookie criminal. All we can do is hope that we
find him in time."

Sydney nodded and gazed out the window
again. Vaughn was wounded and spent. Nadia was
out of commission. Weiss was slowly dying. Her
entire team—her entire *family*—was falling apart.
These people were her world. This had to stop, and
it had to stop now.

I'm going to fix this, Sydney told herself, her
fingers curling tightly around her pen. *I have no
idea how, but I'm going to save Weiss. I owe it to
him. I owe it to all of them.*

Sydney stepped onto the top stair leading from the
plane to the tarmac and the first person she saw
was Marcus Dixon, rushing to meet her. She had
known Dixon long enough to recognize the mixture
of hope and determination in his eyes.

"They have a lead," she said under her breath,
her words all but drowned out by the airport noise
around her. She turned to her sister, who looked

pale and weak, but at least she was awake. She was seated in a wheelchair behind Sydney as the medics prepped to carry her down to the ground. "Are you okay?" Sydney asked.

"Yes. Go," Nadia said. "Find out what's going on."

Sydney raced to the bottom of the stairs and met Dixon. "What's up? Is it Bergin?" she asked.

"You're never going to believe this, but he's back in California," Dixon said, tucking his wind-blown tie into his jacket and buttoning it down. "He was caught on an LAX security camera half an hour ago, badly disguised."

"How did he make it through customs? I thought we flagged him," Sydney said.

"We did, but he was traveling with a well-made fake passport and he made it through," Dixon replied. "Believe me, heads are going to roll. But if you ask me, it's a good thing that he made it out of there."

"How so?" Sydney asked, glancing up at the plane. Vaughn was helping the men escort Nadia to the ground.

"We sent out a couple of agents to tail him," Dixon explained. "He's headed up the coast right now."

Sydney's pulse sped up when she realized what

Dixon was saying. "You think he's leading us to his hiding place," she said. "To the place where he moved all that stuff from his warehouse and the lab in his basement."

"That's my hope," Dixon replied with a nod. "We follow him, we grab the vaccine, we get it to Weiss. It's a lot more efficient than interrogating the guy."

"What's up?" Vaughn asked, joining them as the medics wheeled Nadia over to a waiting ambulance.

"We got Bergin," Sydney replied, trying to temper her elation. She wouldn't feel truly relieved until she had the slippery little scumbag in a holding cell somewhere.

"Two agents are tailing him right now, up near Santa Barbara," Dixon added.

Vaughn's face lit up with anticipation. "Let's go."

Sydney turned and looked at Nadia as they lifted her wheelchair into the back of the ambulance. With one glance she knew that Nadia realized what was going on.

"Go," Nadia mouthed, lifting a hand. *"I'm fine."*

Sydney nodded and followed Dixon and Vaughn to a sleek, black sedan. She would see her sister soon enough. If all went well, the whole group would be together again by sunset.

Two hours later, Dixon pulled the sedan to a stop at the side of a remote, two-way road. Beyond a cliff and down a slope to the left, a small bay sparkled in the midday sunshine. To the right was nothing but trees and rocky terrain. Up ahead, two agents stepped out of a parked car. One was a stocky woman in a no-nonsense pantsuit, with red hair pulled back in a ponytail; the other was a middle-aged man with shaggy blond hair and a paunchy stomach. He hefted up the waistband on his pants as he approached Dixon's vehicle.

"Agent Rhodes," Dixon said, nodding at the male agent as he slammed the car door. "This is Agent Bristow and Agent Vaughn," he said.

"How ya doing?" Agent Rhodes said, lifting a hand over his eyes to shade them from the sun. "This is my partner, Agent Peralta."

Sydney nodded at them both. "What's the status?" she asked, glancing around.

"The suspect drove his rental car down that dirt road about half an hour ago," Agent Rhodes said, pointing at a silt driveway across the street.

"There's a log cabin on the water. He went inside and hasn't moved since. We called it in and were told to wait for you all to get here."

"Does he know you're here?" Dixon asked.

"I doubt it," Agent Peralta said, crossing her arms over her chest. "If he noticed our tail, he didn't show any signs. He seemed pretty distracted and fidgety."

"Sounds like him," Vaughn said.

"So, are we taking this guy in or what?" Rhodes asked. He made an impatient clucking sound with his tongue.

"The plan is to take him into custody and search the premises," Sydney explained, checking her gun and ammo. "We suspect he's moved a large amount of dangerous chemical weapons and virus samples to this location. It's vital that none of these samples be destroyed. We need one of the vaccines to help an agent who has been infected."

"So if this degenerates into a firefight, you don't want it happening in his lab," Agent Peralta said as she slipped on her wire-rimmed sunglasses. "Got it."

"Hopefully it won't come to that," Vaughn told

them. "This guy had a backer who had a lot of firepower, but he was killed last night. As of now, Bergin is just a skittish scientist and he's running scared."

"Sounds like a cakewalk," Agent Rhodes said, slapping a clip into his automatic.

"Still, we should take all the usual precautions," Sydney told them. "This guy has already escaped our grasp twice. We cannot afford to let him get away again."

"Got it," Agent Peralta said.

"Okay, let's spread out," Dixon said, taking charge. "Rhodes, you take the north approach. Peralta and I will come in from the south. Syd, you take the east."

"Got it," Sydney said. She glanced at Vaughn. "You'll wait here and let us know if you see anything?"

Vaughn lifted his sling slightly and smirked. "Sounds about right."

"Everyone, let's keep one another informed of any suspicious movements," Dixon said. "We're all on comm." He looked at Sydney and pulled his gun from his holster. "You ready?" he asked.

Sydney nodded, feeling as if she were coming

around to the homestretch in the longest race of her life. "Let's finish this thing."

The slope leading to the cabin on the water was steep and covered in loose soil. Sydney inched down with her feet parallel to the hill and fought to maintain her footing while still keeping a watchful eye on her surroundings. At the back door of the house was a flat dirt parking lot where Bergin's rented Ford sat next to a beat-up old Jeep. The cabin wall facing Sydney was windowless, but the other three sides of the house were floor-to-ceiling glass, looking out over a deck that ran all the way around the cabin. Bergin would probably be able to spot Dixon and the other agents moving in on him. Sydney was the only one with any kind of cover.

It doesn't matter, Sydney told herself, grasping her gun with both hands as she finally hit level land, twenty yards from the door. *It's just Bergin. The guy is helpless without Land's goons.*

At that moment, a gun was fired and a bullet zoomed past Sydney's arm, shattering a rock on the slope behind her. Heart in her throat, Sydney dove for cover behind the rusty old Jeep as a few more shots rang out.

"We have a shooter on the southern deck," Dixon reported in her ear. "I repeat, we are under fire."

Pressing her back up against the right-front tire, Sydney caught her breath and listened. There were at least three separate guns shooting in various directions. Who the hell did Bergin have protecting him now?

"I have at least one shooter on me," Sydney reported into her comm.

"He's on the northern deck," Agent Rhodes reported, breathless from being under fire as well. "I repeat, Agent Bristow, your shooter is on the northern deck."

Bracing herself, Sydney stood up and caught sight of the gunman. He was standing at the very edge of the deck, leaning around to take aim at the Jeep. She fired off one shot and hit him in the chest. The man screamed in pain and tipped over the handrail on the deck, tumbling down the hill toward the water.

"My shooter is down. I'm at the back door," Sydney told the other agents. "I'm going in."

"Go ahead. We've got this under control," Dixon replied.

Sydney walked up to the wooden door and kicked it in, tearing the latch from the wall. The main level of the cabin was decorated with brown leather couches and chairs, colorful throw rugs, and Native American art. No sign of lab equipment. A set of stairs across the room ran up to a loft, where a bed and lamp took up the entire space. From inside, Sydney could see one guard dead ahead on the deck facing the ocean and another two to the south. A man on the north deck turned around and spotted her inside. His eyes widened and he was about to take aim, but he was shot from behind and fell against the glass, dead.

Thank you, Agent Rhodes, Sydney thought.

Another guard went down, and Sydney knew that Dixon and Peralta had the situation under control. Sydney shoved her gun into the back waistband of her slacks and started to search the room. It didn't look as if anything had been stashed here recently, but she wasn't going to risk missing something. She yanked open a large wooden cabinet and found nothing but books and papers. Another shot was fired, and a bullet shattered one of the windows. Sydney hit the floor instinctively. Her head was still pressed to the woven rug when she heard a crash down below.

Eyes wide, Sydney tried to control her breathing so she could hear. There was definitely another room beneath the floor, and it sounded as if someone was down there making a mess, possibly searching for something. Possibly destroying evidence.

Bergin, Sydney thought.

Lifting her head, she looked around the room. There were no stairs leading down to the basement. She got to her hands and knees, wary of the continued shooting and of making too much noise and alerting whomever was down below. Somewhere in the room there was a latch leading to the lower level. But where?

Then Sydney spotted it. One of the rugs was slightly crumpled, the fringed edge pulled back to expose a wooden knob. She crawled over to it and whipped the rug aside.

Gotcha! she thought, grasping the handle on the small latch. She lifted it up slowly, wincing as it creaked. A sturdy-looking ladder led down to the bottom floor. Unfortunately, the noise down below had stopped. Bergin had either left the room, or had heard her coming and was lying in wait. All she could do was hope that he didn't have a gun. She would be completely vulnerable on her way down the ladder.

Or I could just take the faster route, Sydney thought.

Taking a deep breath, Sydney lowered herself through the hole and dropped to the floor. She stood up and whipped around, gun at the ready, scanning the room. There was no one in sight, but Sydney had hit the mother lode. The place was a wreck, filled with brown boxes stacked into teetering towers. Scientific equipment was strewn everywhere— scales and beakers and microscopes. Clearly, Dixon's hunch had been right. All of Bergin's stuff had been moved here, and it had been moved here in a hurry. Bergin's samples had to be somewhere in this mess. And unless he had escaped yet again, Bergin was here somewhere too.

A few windows set high into the walls afforded some light, and a door across the way most likely opened onto the hillside, affording access to the rocky beach and the water. Outside, the firefight had stopped. The world was silent as Sydney stepped into the center of the room, turning slowly around, waiting for Bergin to make his move. She knew he had either made it out the door before she found the latch, or he was hiding behind one of the stacks of boxes.

Suddenly the door at the side of the room was

kicked open and Sydney whirled around, gun drawn. Dixon stood in the doorway, his chest heaving.

"Is he here?" he asked.

"He was," Sydney replied.

A blinking red light near Dixon's ankle caught her eye, and her heart stopped. "Dixon, what is that?"

He looked down, then shoved a box near his foot aside. Attached to the wall was a small black detonator attached to a wire that ran all the way up the wall and into the ceiling above his head.

"It's gonna blow," he said, his eyes widening with fear. "Everyone, get out of the cabin!" Dixon shouted into his comm. "It's wired to explode!"

Sydney tore out the side door and ran across the slope, getting as far away from the house as possible. The force of the explosion knocked her forward, off her feet, and Dixon dove on top of her, shielding her from the fire and debris. Together they rolled down the hill and came to rest on the rocky shore just a few feet from the waves.

"Are you all right?" Dixon asked.

"Yeah," Sydney replied hollowly, sitting up on her elbows. Bergin's cabin was a ball of flames. "It was in there somewhere. The vaccine was in there."

Dixon hung his head, catching his breath. Bergin had not just destroyed his life's work. He had also just destroyed their last chance at saving Weiss.

"Sydney! Dixon! Are you guys all right?" Vaughn said in Sydney's ear.

"We're fine," Sydney replied.

"Peralta? Rhodes?" Dixon asked.

"We're okay. We're together," Peralta replied. "I don't think we're taking anyone into custody, though."

Sydney swallowed back a lump in her throat. It was over. The mission, Weiss's life. It was all over.

Somewhere, beyond the sounds of shattering glass and *whooshing* flames, Sydney heard another noise. It was the sputtering sound of a small engine revving to life, but it wasn't coming from the car park. Those cars had been incinerated. The noise was coming from the opposite direction.

"Do you hear that?" Sydney asked, scrambling to her feet.

"Hear what?" Dixon asked.

"It's a boat," Sydney said, her pulse shifting into hyperdrive. "He has a boat."

She took off at a sprint, across the rocks and toward the burning house.

"Sydney! What are you doing?" Dixon cried. "Get back here!"

At that point, there wasn't anyone in the world who could've stopped Sydney. She jumped down from a rocky ledge onto the slim strip of sand below. There, pushing away from a dock at the foot of the hill, was Dr. Lance Bergin. He sat down at the helm of a small speedboat. A small speedboat loaded down with metal boxes.

He still has his samples, she thought. *He still has the vaccine!*

"Bergin! Stop!" Sydney shouted.

He glanced over his shoulder, spotted her, and hit the gas, bouncing over the small waves and out into the open bay.

Sydney whirled around and saw that Dixon was hot on her heels. "We have to go after him! He has the vaccine!" Sydney shouted.

Together, Sydney and Dixon raced for the dock. The remaining boat tethered there was an older model, but it was their only option. Sydney hoped that the added weight of Bergin's samples would slow him down enough for her and Dixon to catch up.

Dixon untied the rope from the dock, and

Sydney revved the engine. Luckily the boat was gassed up and ready to go.

"Hang on!" she shouted.

Dixon braced himself, and Sydney pushed the throttle forward, almost knocking herself off her feet.

We have power, Sydney thought as the wind whipped her hair around her face. Bergin had turned his boat north and was now speeding along the coastline, kicking up substantial wakes and earning angry shouts from the fishing boats he was racing past. Sydney leaned farther into the throttle, pushing it to its limits. The fishermen were just going to have to relax. She had a friend to save.

"You're gaining on him," Dixon said, blinking against the spray and the sun.

Bergin glanced over his shoulder and his eyes widened when he saw Sydney hot on his trail. He cut the wheel left, speeding right toward an idling boat where a water-skier was setting himself up.

"What the hell is he doing?" Sydney shouted, following Bergin at top speed.

Bergin swerved, narrowly missing the back of the boat pulling the water-skier, and Sydney followed after him.

"He thinks you won't follow him if you're putting other people in danger," Dixon told her.

Yeah, well, think again, Sydney thought.

Bergin dodged around a few more anchored boats, ripping the fishing rod right out of one man's hand and knocking another woman off her skiff with his wake. Sydney didn't back off. In fact, by the time he was done with his little obstacle course, she had caught up to the point where she could pull up alongside of him.

"Stop the boat!" Dixon shouted.

Bergin huddled close to the wheel and tried to speed up.

"Stop the boat!" Dixon shouted again.

Up ahead, Sydney saw a wide stretch of beach, void of sunbathers thanks to a huge population of seagulls feasting on washed-up crustaceans. Suddenly, she had a plan. She pushed her boat even harder, edging ahead of Bergin.

"What are you doing?" Dixon asked.

"I'm gonna run him aground," she replied.

"What?" Dixon shouted. "You're going to get us all killed."

"Trust me," she said.

Gradually, Sydney edged her boat to the right,

toward Bergin's. He pulled to the right as well, trying to avoid her. But Sydney kept bearing down on him until Bergin was forced to slow his engine and turn farther and farther to the right.

"Are you crazy?" he shouted as they sped directly toward the shoreline.

Sydney ignored him and kept going. The beach was a hundred yards away now. Bergin slowed further and Sydney did the same, but not by much. Fifty yards. Thirty. The birds started to scatter. Dixon sat down and braced his arms against the wall and the seat next to him. Twenty yards.

"Hang on!" Sydney shouted.

The boats slammed into the shore at the same time and bounced up onto the rocks and sand and shells. Startled seagulls squawked and took flight, exploding into the air in all directions. Every bone in Sydney's body was jarred, but she flung herself out of the vessel as soon as it stopped and raced over to Bergin. He was clinging breathlessly to the wheel of his boat, a sizable cut on his forehead, his eyes wild. Sydney was relieved to see that he had secured the boxes in the back.

Sydney drew her gun and pointed it directly at Bergin's chest.

"I just wanted to save my samples," Bergin said, raising his hands shakily. "Land told me to destroy everything if anything happened to him, but I couldn't destroy my life's work."

"Do you have the VX411 vaccine on this boat?" Sydney demanded.

Bergin glanced at his boxes.

"Do you have it?" Sydney shouted.

"If . . . if I give it to you . . . will you let me go?" Bergin asked. "I mean, can we make some kind of deal here?"

I guess you have it, then, Sydney thought. She shoved her gun into the waistband of her pants, pulled back, and slammed her fist across Bergin's face, knocking him out cold.

"Sydney! What are you doing?" Dixon shouted, running up next to her.

They looked down at Bergin, who was slumped over the front of his boat. "He is *not* getting away from me this time," Sydney said.

CHAPTER 14

Sydney stood by Weiss's side, holding his cold, lifeless hand while the vaccine was administered. She watched the clear liquid disappear as it was injected into his bloodstream.

Please don't let it be too late, she thought.

The doctor placed the syringe on a sterilized towel and turned to Sydney, her face lined with doubt. "All we can do now is wait," she said.

Sydney nodded. "What are his chances?"

"I wish I could tell you," the doctor said with a sigh. "He's been in critical condition for forty-eight hours. We're not sure his body is going to be able to recover. We'll just have to—"

"I know," Sydney said in a soft tone, looking down at Weiss. "Wait and see."

The doctor nodded and slipped from the room. Sydney pulled up a chair and sat next to Weiss's bed. She squeezed his hand, and tears welled up in her eyes.

"You have to get well," she said. "We need you around here."

She looked up and wiped at her cheeks as Vaughn stepped into the room. He gave her a small, reassuring smile and ran his hand over her hair. Suddenly, Sydney felt able to breathe again.

"Just got finished with Bergin," Vaughn said. "He told Land that he had moved everything to his cabin, so Land sent those men to protect the place. Apparently those guys didn't even know that their boss was dead."

"Breakdown in communication, huh?" Sydney joked.

"Well, the good news is, we have all of Bergin's samples now, including what was left of the VX411," Vaughn told her. "Dr. Moskowitz is going over Bergin's notes, and apparently he really has made some strides with AIDS and Alzheimer's. They're going to send his research to the appropriate labs so they can get to work on his findings."

"I guess there are two sides to everyone," Sydney said with a sigh, leaning her head against Vaughn's hip.

He draped his arm lightly over her shoulder. "At least it's all over now,"

Sydney took a deep breath and looked at Weiss's pale, stubble-covered cheek. "Not totally."

Vaughn tugged at Sydney's hair, and she looked up at him, attempting to smile. "You look exhausted," he said. "You should go home and get some rest."

"No, I don't think I could sleep," Sydney said, even though her aching muscles and joints told her otherwise. She stretched and leaned back in her chair. "I think I'll stay here tonight."

"Okay, then," Vaughn said, slipping his suit jacket off. "I'll stay too."

He drew up another chair and draped his jacket over Sydney's shoulders. She smiled and pulled it closer to her, relishing the warmth. It was going to be a long night of worrying and waiting, but she was glad Vaughn was here to share it with her. Together they settled in and hoped for a miracle.

A sudden jolt startled Sydney awake and she lifted her head so fast, her vision clouded over with a fuzzy gray haze. She blinked a couple of times and brought her hand to her neck, which had developed a nasty knot. Groaning, she tipped her head back and rolled it, trying to work out the tightness.

"Good morning."

Sydney's heart skipped a beat. She glanced at Vaughn, who was passed out in the chair next to her with his head lolling back and his legs sprawled out in front of him. Then, hoping against hope, she looked at Eric.

His eyes were open. He was smiling. He was alive.

"You're okay!" Sydney said, her heart expanding.

"Yeah, but I could use some water," Weiss croaked. "What kind of nurse are you?"

Sydney jumped on Weiss and hugged him so hard, he grunted.

"Okay, still a little fragile over here," he said, patting her back.

"Sorry. Sorry," she said, standing. "I'm just so happy to have you back."

She grabbed the water pitcher off the table near the wall and poured him a cup. "Should we wake him up?" Sydney said, lifting her chin toward Vaughn as she handed the water to Weiss.

"Nah. I like to hear him snore," Weiss replied. He sipped at his water, then put the cup on the swinging tray next to his bed. He looked up at Sydney mischievously. "On the count of three."

Sydney smirked and nodded.

"One . . . two . . . three—"

"Vaughn!" they both shouted.

He gave a full body twitch and lurched out of his chair. Sydney and Weiss cracked up laughing as he recovered and took in the scene.

"That was so not funny," he said, holding one hand over his heart. Then he looked at Weiss, and his eyes lit up. "You're awake."

"Yeah, buddy!" Weiss said. "Thanks to you guys, I assume."

Vaughn pushed himself to his feet and leaned down to hug Weiss. Sydney stood back, hands in the back pockets of her jeans, watching the reunion with relief and joy. Everything was going to be okay. She had messed up on her mission—royally—and she was sure she would hear all about it from Sloane.

But for now, all that mattered was that Weiss was okay. That was all she cared about.

"I've never been so happy to see someone wake up in my entire life," Vaughn said.

Eric smiled, his eyes full of happiness and the realization of how close he had come to death. "Yeah, well," he said, "I've never been so happy to be awake."

"I've brought you all here to congratulate you on a job well done," Sloane said, taking everyone in his office by surprise.

Marshall and Vaughn exchanged a confused glance. Nadia shifted uncomfortably in her wheelchair, which she would be confined to for a couple of weeks while doing rehab on her leg. Dixon raised one eyebrow at Sydney as Sloane paced before them.

"Land is dead," Sloane continued. "Bergin is in the custody of the CIA, and we have all of his samples—the good *and* the bad. And, as you all know, Agent Weiss is on his way to a full recovery."

Sloane paused in front of his desk. "But, although I am pleased with the ultimate results, I am far less than pleased with the way in which this mission was handled."

Ah. Here it is, Sydney thought.

"You are all aware of the number of mistakes that our team committed on this mission. I won't embarrass you by reading the list," Sloane said, looking at each one of them in turn. "But I hope that you have all learned from your experiences in the field these past few days, and that knowledge has strengthened our team."

Sydney smiled slightly and looked at Vaughn. What had really strengthened their team was getting Weiss back.

"But let me put you on notice right now," Sloane said firmly. "This division cannot function if we all conduct ourselves like a bunch of irresponsible, selfish schoolchildren. I will not tolerate another incident like this."

Sydney bit her tongue to keep from saying something sarcastic. Right now was not the time to get into it with Sloane. Eric was waiting for them.

"You are dismissed," Sloane said.

Everyone stood up and quickly left the room. Marshall helped Nadia maneuver her wheelchair around the skinny metal legs of the couches and chairs.

"Leave it to Sloane to turn a victory party into a

scolding," Vaughn said, shoving his hands in his pockets as they all headed to the elevators as a group.

"Forget him," Marshall said, reaching out to stab the button with his finger. "He's not gonna harsh my vibe."

Sydney looked around at the group, and they all tried to hide their laughter—unsuccessfully.

"What?" Marshall said as the elevator doors slid open. "You guys just aren't down with the current slang."

The laughter exploded as they stepped into the elevator and the doors closed again. Sydney loved this feeling. Everyone was happy, everyone was healthy, there was no guilt or pressure hanging over any of them. It was one of those rare moments when she felt free.

Weiss's room was already prepped for their arrival. The patient had bribed his nurses and doctors into decorating it with colorful streamers and balloons. A stereo played dance music in the corner and Weiss was propped up in his bed, wearing a red silk robe over his hospital gown and a gaudy gold crown on his head.

"Welcome to the Weiss Lives party!" he shouted, throwing his arms wide.

Marshall and Nadia cheered and Sydney clapped her hands, getting into the spirit.

"Can I get the guest of honor some soda?" she asked, crossing to a drink table set up near his bed.

"Yes. Grape, please," he said. "Only the best."

Sydney laughed and placed a couple of ice cubes into a cup. Marshall poured out a few sodas for the rest of the group and passed them around. Sydney poured Weiss's drink and handed it to him.

"So . . . listen . . . I never really got to apologize for what happened," she said. Over in the corner, Vaughn turned up the music and Marshall did a hammed-up version of the running man, cracking up Nadia and Dixon.

Weiss took a sip of his drink, and his brow creased. "What? At the lab?"

"Yeah," Sydney said, toying with the edge of his blanket. "I should have kept a better eye on Bergin. I should have—"

"Wait, wait, wait, wait, wait," Weiss said, waving a hand around. "Please tell me you have not been beating yourself up over what happened."

Sydney nodded, ashamed and embarrassed.

"Syd, it could have easily been the other way around," Weiss said. "If you had gone for the computer and I had been searching for the vials, you would be in this bed right now."

Sydney tried to meet his eye.

Finally she had to give in—if anyone had a right to blame Sydney for making mistakes during the mission, it was Weiss, and he obviously didn't hold her responsible. It was time to accept her faults and move on. "Okay, okay. You're right," she said finally. "Thanks, Weiss."

"Anytime," he said. "Now would you get me some Doritos already?"

Sydney joined the crowd of agents near the food. Vaughn was chowing down on chips and pretzels. "You might wanna bring some of that to the big man," Sydney told him. "He's very demanding."

"I'm on it," Vaughn said, walking off with a couple of bowls of snacks. Dixon grabbed the popcorn and joined him.

"Marshall, do you mind if I talk to Nadia alone for a minute?" Sydney asked, feeling a twist of nervousness in her stomach. Nadia looked up at her questioningly.

"Uh, sure," Marshall said, placing a party hat on his head and snapping the elastic. "Ow. I, uh, really need to change this music, anyway."

He headed off for the stereo, and Sydney pulled up a chair next to Nadia. "I owe you an apology," she said, tucking her hair behind her ear. "Several apologies, actually."

"Sydney, that's not necessary," Nadia said.

"Yes, it is. I've been thinking about it all day and I realized that I've been feeling a little . . . resentful of your presence on the team," Sydney said, swallowing hard.

"Resentful," Nadia repeated.

"It's not as bad as it sounds," Sydney told her quickly. "It's just that I've been the only woman in this boys' club for so long that I just got used to it. What I didn't realize was how important it had become to me. To the way I define myself—if that makes any sense."

She glanced at Nadia, who nodded slightly, encouraging her to continue.

"I think your being here . . . taking over the mission . . . I think it just threw me a little," she said.

"You felt expendable," Nadia said softly.

There was a sharp pain in Sydney's heart, but she brushed it aside. "Yeah, I guess I did. But it's no excuse for the way I've been acting. I shouldn't have tried to tell you what to do, and I'm sorry I've been so short-tempered."

"Please, Sydney," Nadia said. "You were no more short-tempered than usual."

Sydney smiled.

"I'm sorry if I've made you uncomfortable," Nadia said. "It was never my intention to come in here and disrupt your life."

"You haven't," Sydney said earnestly. "You've made my life better. And to be honest, it might be nice to have another woman around to take the pressure off. And to diffuse all the testosterone."

Nadia laughed, and they both glanced across the room at the four men who were now gathered around Weiss's bed, playing with the PlayStation he had requested that morning.

"It's nice to have an ally in the boys' club," Sydney said with a smile.

"Here," Nadia said, handing Sydney a full cup of soda. She picked up another from the table and held it up. "To the girls' club," she said, just as the boys erupted in cheers for some ridiculous virtual slam dunk Weiss had just made.

Sydney smiled and clicked cups with Nadia. "I'll drink to that."

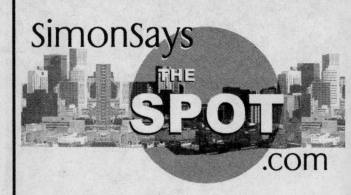